"IF I'D HAD ANY IDEA HOW MUCH YOUR HAREBRAINED SCHEME WAS GOING TO UPSET OUR LIVES, I'D NEVER HAVE FUNDED IT."

Stunned at his words, Mariah fell back against the leather couch.

"Harebrained scheme?" she challenged. "As I recall, you were right in there every minute with your suggestions for PCs and logos and all those other things I'd never heard of."

"I wanted to make sure you didn't have to go back to the cocktail circuit," David explained. "I couldn't stand the idea of other men making drunken passes at you."

"So," Mariah said, her eyes narrowing, "you thought you could buy me. You're so jealous nothing else matters. Well, I have news for you. You'll never own me . . . never . . ."

CANDLELIGHT ECSTASY CLASSIC ROMANCES

WHAT EVERY WOMAN WANTS

Blair Cameron

A CANDLELIGHT ECSTASY ROMANCE®

Published by
Dell Publishing Co., Inc.
1 Dag Hammarskjold Plaza
New York, New York 10017

ISBN: 0-440-19444-X

Printed in the United States of America

September 1987

10 9 8 7 6 5 4 3 2 1

WFH

To Our Readers:

As of September 1987, Candlelight Romances will cease publication of Candlelight Ecstasies and Supremes. The editors of Candlelight would like to thank our readers for 20 years of loyalty and support. Providing quality romances has been a wonderful experience for us and one we will cherish. Again, from everyone at Candlelight, thank you!

Sincerely,

The Editors

WHAT EVERY
WOMAN WANTS

CHAPTER ONE

Mariah Benedict resignedly shifted her weight from one slim hip to the other. For almost half an hour she'd been stuck in the middle line of three that extended the entire length of the Vehicle Licensing Department. Although she knew it was impossible, it seemed to her that for each persevering person who left triumphantly, registration tags in hand, at least two more came in. Mariah had to smile at the common look of exasperation that spread across the newcomers' faces, even though she was in the same boat. She watched as their anxious gazes scanned the lines in the futile hope of finding one shorter than another.

To be fair, Mariah thought with a feeble attempt at humor, the city should inscribe the words, "All hope abandon, ye who enter here," below the name of the department that was painted on the corridor side of the doors. No one had any hopes of getting out of this place in a reasonable amount of time. Rubbing her hand over the small of her back, she fought off a dreary sense of fatigue.

Bored with the momentary diversion of glancing around the room, Mariah's gaze settled once more upon the beguiling back of the muscular man standing directly in front of her. For the first restless while she'd spent in the slow-moving line, the man's back had been merely a back, nothing more than another time-consuming obstruction between her and the clerk at the counter. But as the minutes had ticked by and her gaze had rested on the massive planes and contours of the body that effectively blocked her view of the rest of the line, she'd gradually become aware that something deep inside her was responding pleasurably to his blatant maleness. So for the last twenty minutes or more she'd stood entranced by the way the clean white T-shirt, glowing in the harsh fluorescent light, stretched snugly across his amazingly broad shoulders, then narrowed pleasingly to fit around a trim waist before disappearing into the low-slung waistline of his jeans.

Inch by inch her eyes had taken in the latent power suggested in his deeply tanned arms, burnished with golden hairs that glistened in the artificial light of the windowless room. It was nearly criminal the way her hands itched to reach up and tangle themselves in the heavy sun-bleached blond hair that curled enticingly at the back of his sturdy neck.

After memorizing every detail of the man's fascinating back, from the muscular bulges of his brawny thighs to the way his vibrant mane swirled around the cowlick on his well-shaped head, Mariah longed to know if his flip side could possibly match the incredible impression his hit side had made on her senses.

Confident in the easy manner natural to her warm personality, Mariah raised to her tiptoes and spoke toward the shoulder that loomed inches above her own five-foot-seven-inch height. "How much longer

10

do you think we're going to be in this line?" she asked.

The sight of the handsome sun-bronzed face that turned toward her nearly took her breath away. The brush of straight brows above his wide sea-green eyes was only slightly darker than the shock of blond hair that waved across his broad forehead. His even white teeth flashed as he answered, "Each transaction has taken about five minutes so far. I'd estimate another forty minutes before I make it to the counter. Minimum."

The unsettling intent look of his deepset eyes met the mesmerized stare of her own clear gray ones for a long moment, a moment in which Mariah felt her heart lurch peculiarly. Her full lips curved unwittingly into a wry smile as she realized that she would be unable to identify which was his hit side, since the view of the front was as spectacularly attractive as his back.

"Look," his deep melodious voice continued as he held up a sheaf of envelopes, "I have several vehicles to register and that's going to take quite a while even after I get up there. Why don't you get in front of me?" He courteously stepped aside to allow her to pass.

For a second Mariah was tempted to accept his invitation. But the thought of not being able to observe his stalwart dimensions, coupled with the logical reasoning that she really had nowhere else that she had to be, kept her in her place.

Mariah smiled, shaking her head. "What's one more line to me today? I'm sure you have more to do with your time than I have." A note of wistfulness shaded her truthful reply.

"A woman of leisure?" he asked.

Confirming her suspicion that he'd moved back only to get a better view of her, his sea-green gaze traveled over her hair and face. Tensing, Mariah consciously straightened her casual pose. Only the telltale beat at the base of her slender throat threatened to reveal her inner turmoil as his eyes followed the smooth lines of the fashionably oversized white jacket she'd belted around her slim waist. Lazily continuing its unhurried path, his interested gaze took in the flare of the skirt of her scarlet and white sundress, stopping its appraisal only when it reached the polished tips of her tanned bare feet in their stylish red sandals.

"That's one way of putting it, I suppose," she answered with a rueful grin, thinking that although it had made her decidedly uncomfortable, she had to admit turn-about was fair play. She'd certainly spent enough time looking at him to allow him his scrutiny of her. Seeing a puzzled expression fleetingly cross his striking features she explained, "I'm between jobs right now—with a lot more leisure than I can afford."

When a look of sympathy entered his eyes, Mariah shrugged her shoulders in what she hoped was an offhanded manner. An unaccountable urge to confide in him made her add, "This is par for the course for me. I waited in line for an hour and a half at the unemployment office and now it looks as if I'll probably be here at least that long. Then it's on to the regular Friday lineup at the bank to deposit my check. Add to that an exciting trip to the supermarket where I'll spend far more time in line than I will picking out my groceries. Then I'm off to a cut-rate service station where half the city will be gassing up

12

for the weekend. And after that I'll be caught in rush-hour traffic, creeping along until I finally reach my exit. By then my whole day will be down the drain, spent just waiting to be waited on! Do I sound sorry for myself?" she asked, suddenly worried at having been so frank.

"Nope." The tall man grinned at her. "You just sound like a realist to me. I like that. No sugar coating, just the plain facts. Why did you lose your job, if you don't mind my asking?"

"I don't mind," Mariah said, somehow pleased that he was interested. "My last job was at King Lucky's. I lost my job when the club folded."

"What did you do there? Keep the books?"

"Hardly," Mariah chuckled wryly, "although they might still be in business if I had. I've been a cocktail waitress since the day I turned twenty-one. I've seen more lounges close their doors because of poor management than you'd believe. I'm really tired of that whole scene."

At her words, David Anthony's mind's eye transformed the casually dressed, good-looking young woman standing before him into a dazzlingly glamorous creature. He pictured her long, curly blond hair flowing down over a low-cut shimmering gold lamé blouse that emphasized the swell of her high, firm breasts. And with the slim ankles that he'd managed to get a look at, he instinctively knew that her legs would be terrific in a pair of black mesh stockings below a short satin skirt. Suddenly a feeling close to jealousy spread over him at the realization that other men had actually seen her lithe figure in a costume similar to that he'd imagined, and even

13

more disturbing, many had undoubtedly made drunken passes at her.

"Maybe you'll be able to find something different to do," he suggested.

"I sure hope so," Mariah admitted. "Being on unemployment is really demoralizing. I may be kidding myself, but I like to think that I'm a person with drive and ambition. I keep telling myself that I'm through with being a cocktail waitress, but I don't know if I can pull it off. All the job interviews I've been sent on were dismal failures because I just don't have the skills to do anything else."

"Maybe you should try going back to school," he suggested helpfully.

Mariah shook her head. "I'm not sure I can cut it. I tried that a few years ago and I didn't get anywhere. I was too tired from working half the night to even get up in time for my classes, much less study for them. It was really frustrating. I felt like a total failure. But maybe I should try again," she added without conviction.

"If you seriously want to make a change, you might try setting goals for yourself and sticking to them. That's always worked for me. Just take it a step at a time and hang in there," he remarked, a reassuring smile lighting his eyes. "You look to me like a woman who's going to make it."

"Thanks. I'll try," Mariah answered. Something in his empathetic sea-green eyes buoyed her confidence. A tiny constriction circled her heart as a flush tinted her cheeks. There was nothing tentative about this man. Boldly physical, he was clearly a man of action and resolve.

Not wanting the conversation to end, but needing

to change the focus from herself, Mariah commented, "You know, I just can't understand the number of people waiting in here. I know why I'm here. I didn't have the money or I would have mailed in a check long ago and spared myself this wait. It's a good thing I'm used to being on my feet.

"But look at these people," she gestured toward the silent, grim-faced individuals around her. Many of the men were dressed in business suits, rocking impatiently on the heels of costly, freshly shined shoes. Others, like the man before her, were dressed in worn jeans and T-shirts, and glanced repeatedly at their watches as they shifted their weight from one sturdy leg to the other. The women in their crisp summer clothing were as restive as the men.

"It's obvious they all have somewhere else they'd rather be. And most of them look like they would have had enough money in their checking accounts to have let them mail in for their license tags weeks ago. Why do you think they're here?"

"You've got me," he answered. "I hadn't even thought about it. I suppose there are as many reasons as there are people. I'm here because the secretary at the office was supposed to have taken care of this before she went on her honeymoon," he stated with a tinge of annoyance. "But she was too love-struck those last few weeks before the wedding to get anything done. I found these under her blotter this morning when I was digging through her desk looking for the tags."

Mariah grinned. "You don't seem to have much use for anyone who lets affairs of the heart come before business. It takes time and a lot of thought to plan a beautiful wedding."

15

"She only worked eight hours a day," he answered with mock gruffness, a glint of humor in his eyes. "That still left her sixteen for her personal life."

"My goodness," Mariah teased. "You sound like you're a slave driver."

"I just don't like it when I have to do other people's jobs for them," he retorted easily. His eyes were now alight with amusement. "I don't have time for that sort of thing. I'm far too busy keeping my crews' noses to the grindstone. And right now that's where I need to be."

Reaching out to take her left hand which he quickly noted was free of a wedding band, he raised it and the white envelope it held to eye level. "Ms. Mariah Benedict," he read the name it was addressed to, "I've got a proposition for you. If you honestly have the time, I'd appreciate your buying my tags for me, because I was only half kidding. I do have plenty to do with my time. I had to leave a crew of men working on a hundred-and-forty-unit apartment complex to come over here. And since I'm the," he hesitated a fraction of a moment before supplying the word, "foreman, I need to get back on the job. So, how about it? Will you help me out? I'll be happy to pay you for your services."

"I don't know," Mariah said uncertainly, feeling a pleasant tingling caused by the touch of his large-boned, callus-roughened hands. "Do you really think I can do that for you without causing some kind of snafu?"

"Sure. Why not? The check is made out to the license bureau, and I've got the registration forms for each vehicle right here."

He slid the envelopes he held into her hand before

reaching into his back pocket for his wallet and opening it. "I'd appreciate it if you'd do it for me."

The heart-wrenching smile that accompanied his declaration convinced Mariah that there was absolutely nothing she'd rather do at the moment than stand in line to buy this man's tags for him.

"Here's the check, a little something for your effort, and my business card," he remarked matter-of-factly, taking the items from his wallet before sliding them on top of the stack of envelopes she held.

"But where do you want the tags delivered?" she asked, glancing down at the address on the envelope that was half obscured by the items he'd added to the pile. She could just make out the words "Construction Company."

"I'll pick them up when I get off work." He moved out of the line, taking a few steps back as he pushed his wallet back into his pocket.

"But you don't know where I live," she called out plaintively.

"Got a mind like a steel trap," he assured her, smiling and tapping his finger against his golden temple. "I saw your address on your registration when I read your name. See you tonight."

Mariah watched in stunned silence as he strode toward the door with easy confident strides, pushed the swinging panel open, and left the crowded room without a backward glance.

With a small shock of surprise she realized that even though they'd shared a conversation that touched on very personal aspects of her life, she didn't even know the gorgeous blond man's name. Sorting through the papers in her hand, Mariah learned from the business card that he was a builder

17

named David Anthony, who worked for the Superior Construction Company, and an examination of the envelopes told her that the six vehicles she was registering for him belonged to Superior. The large check was bank certified and had been signed by a Ruth Owens, secretary for the construction company. The two bills he'd added to the pile were crisp new twenties. Looking at the money a strange uneasiness gripped her. Should she have accepted so much cash from such an attractive man for such an unorthodox reason?

"Miss." Mariah felt a light tap on her shoulder, interrupting her disturbing thoughts.

Turning around she looked into the anxious face of a trim, gray-haired woman.

"Yes?"

"I'm Angela Worth. I couldn't help but overhear your conversation with that young man. I wonder if you'd mind buying my registration tags for me? You see, I work here in the county-city building and I thought I could just run in and take care of this on my lunch hour, but the lines have moved so slowly that I'm not going to make it. I'm a court reporter and I'm due in a hearing in less than ten minutes. If I'm even one minute late," she glanced nervously at the wall clock, "Judge Bradley will have my head."

Without waiting for a response, the woman continued, "Here's my check and registration. You can deliver the tags to the Probate Court Office, room 137." Then, eyeing the bills in Mariah's hand she asked, "Would ten dollars be all right?"

Before Mariah could answer, the woman had opened her clutch purse and was offering the bill.

Why not? Mariah asked herself. Obviously this was

something the woman badly needed done, and why shouldn't she accept money for performing the service? Suddenly she felt more comfortable about the money David Anthony had given her. After all, her time *was* worth something.

"I'd be happy to do it for you, but from the looks of things," she gestured toward the line of people still looming in front of her, "it will be quite a while before I can deliver your tags."

"Don't I know it!" the woman exclaimed. "My husband, Pete, thinks it's ridiculous, but I try to save on postage whenever I can. And every year I tell myself that I'll get in here before the deadline, but I just can't make myself do it." She lowered her voice confidentially. "If that husband of mine ever found out how economical this little 'economy' of mine has turned out to be, I'd never hear the end of it! He'd die laughing if he knew that trying to save twenty-two cents had cost me ten dollars. I just wish I'd known sooner that you'd do this for me so I could have eaten my lunch.

"Mike, come over here," Angela Worth's strident voice called out to a well-dressed man that she beckoned from another line. "This nice young woman has agreed to get my tags for me. Why don't you have her get yours, too?"

Then, as the young man walked toward them, Angela confided to Mariah in a low voice, "Mike is one of the lawyers on the case I'm assigned to. He's due back in court the same time I am."

"Just give her your registration and a signed check, and she can leave your tags in my office when she delivers mine," Angela ordered the attorney with a mother-hen bossiness that the young man obeyed.

19

Mariah answered the tolerant amusement that sparkled from his deep brown eyes with a grin.

"Is this lady licensed and bonded, Angela?" he joked as he wrote out the check.

"Michael, don't be silly. Young attorneys," Angela remarked to Mariah with feigned exasperation. "They think they know it all.

"Now," Angela directed, "give her ten dollars for her time and trouble."

Mariah noted with something close to astonishment that this request didn't cause so much as a raised eyebrow on the attorney's handsome face. He readily offered her two five-dollar bills.

"Thanks, I really appreciate this. It's a heck of a lot cheaper than paying a fine for being found in contempt of court," Mike called over his shoulder as he was urged along by the formidable court reporter.

By the time Mariah left the Bureau of Licensing her step was light. The sense of fatigue that had earlier threatened to overcome her had completely dissipated. She was eighty dollars richer and had, for the first time in weeks, the marvelous feeling of having accomplished something with her time.

And even better, an idea was beginning to take shape in her mind. An idea that might very well change her entire future. It had never occurred to her before today that there might be people who would be willing, even eager, to pay someone to stand in line to perform mundane tasks for them. Would there be enough call for a service like that to turn it into a business? she wondered as she walked down the marble corridor. It was something to think about.

After delivering the two sets of tags to room 137, Mariah strode briskly to the parking lot. Opening the doors and windows of her ancient Dodge Dart, she aired the stuffy heat out of her un-air-conditioned car. She still had two more sets of tags to deliver to other people who had commissioned her to perform the same service for them before she braved the other lines that faced her during the long afternoon.

At least the trip to the supermarket would be fun this time instead of the dreary task it had become. She would be able to afford more than her usual noodle soup and boxed macaroni and cheese. As she drove along, she mentally listed the groceries she would need for the dinner for two she planned to have waiting when David Anthony came to pick up his tags.

After he had gone, the forty minutes she'd spent waiting in line had passed much more quickly than she'd expected. It had been as though meeting him had added a new dimension to her life. The flatness, the feelings of unfulfillment that had plagued her in recent months had been replaced with a curious expectancy that had left her body tingling with a warm glow. She supposed she had met other men who were as attractive as he, but she couldn't remember who or when. In their all too brief encounter David Anthony had intrigued her, had piqued her imagination, had stirred her senses. She had found herself inexplicably drawn to him.

It was during the wait that she'd hit on the idea of preparing dinner for him. She wanted to get to know him better, wanted the chance to see him again and talk over with him the vague idea that had been forming in her mind. After all, it had been his suggestion that he pay her to get the tags that had started the little wheels in her brain moving.

Every detail of the meal had to be perfect. Her heart sang with excitement as she thought of the thick steaks she would choose, and the fresh vegetables she'd select with care. And this would be an ideal time to make her favorite potato casserole. She suspected David Anthony was a meat and potatoes kind of guy, and that was fine with her, but tonight there would be special meat and special potatoes for a special guy. She wasn't ordinarily superstitious, but somehow finding herself eighty dollars richer only a few moments after meeting him had seemed like a sign that her luck was about to change. She owed him a dinner even if her feelings proved wrong and next week she was back living on macaroni and cheese. For the moment she was happy, and it was all because of him.

Wait just a minute, she told herself, braking to stop for a light. He had said he was dropping by after work to pick up the tags. Maybe he'd be on his way home to a wife—even kids. She had no way of knowing whether or not he was married, but realistically chances were that he was. The attractive men usually were. She was so accustomed to being wary of and diligent in warding off advances from married men that she couldn't for the life of her imagine why that possibility had not occurred to her when it came to David Anthony.

Why hadn't she had the good sense to work that crucial question into their first conversation? she asked herself as she listlessly pressed on the accelerator. Because she hadn't known he would suddenly make the unusual proposal that would lead to seeing him again that evening. Feeling suddenly as deflated as an abandoned beachball, she resolved to buy two steaks anyhow. She could always wait and see how things went before offering him dinner. Besides, after the meager diet she'd lived on for the past few weeks, if David Anthony was a married man and had to be on his way, she could eat them both herself!

CHAPTER TWO

The sun was setting in a red haze that stretched across the western horizon, silhouetting the snow-capped Olympic Mountains, when David Anthony got out of his battered pickup on a tree-lined street in a quiet old neighborhood in east Seattle. Crossing the lawn in a few long-legged strides, he whistled cheerfully as he bounded up the steps of the covered porch of the converted mansion whose house number matched the one he'd memorized from Mariah Benedict's registration envelope. Bending down to read the names beside the various buzzers, he firmly pressed his forefinger on the one labeled Benedict-304.

Once inside the solid mahogany entry door, his hand appraised the sturdy, massive oak bannister as his feet climbed the wide, carpeted treads of the well-built staircase that curved up the center of the old house. They didn't make them like this anymore, he thought as he ascended the first flight.

Hearing a door open on the top floor, another flight above him, he looked up to catch sight of Mariah's golden hair cascading down as she peered over the railing to see who had rung her buzzer. He quickened his steps at the sight of her friendly face and welcoming smile.

"Hi there," he called warmly as he rapidly closed the distance between them.

"Hello," Mariah answered with a subdued reserve, noticing once again his complete handsomeness, checking each detail against the image she'd carried with her all day. The open-necked polo shirt and casual slacks he wore did nothing to detract from the appeal of his magnificent physique. Oh, please, let him not be married, she willed with all her might. Her thoughts were so intense that for one terrible second she was afraid she'd spoken them aloud.

"Come on in," she invited cautiously as he reached her floor. "I'll get the tags for you. Frankly I'd almost given you up." Why did she say that? she asked herself, biting her tongue. There was no way she wanted David Anthony to know how anxious she had been to see him again.

"I tried to call you," he said as he closed the door behind him and saw the most unique studio apartment he'd ever seen. "But you weren't listed in the book."

"I had to get an unlisted number," she answered warily, keeping a watchful eye on his expression. "Too many crank calls. Calls from married men. Things like that." His face remained blandly innocent, she noted with a repressed sigh of relief.

"Well, it's a good idea, I guess." He nodded his approval. "You're a lot safer that way."

Assailed by the sweet scent of her perfume, a strong wave of desire surged over him. He needed a woman in his life, he realized suddenly. Once in a while he'd felt a stab of loneliness, but he thought he had left all ability to care deeply for a woman in that impersonal divorce court years before. His self-imposed bachelorhood hadn't really bothered him until that afternoon, when he'd become obsessed with thoughts of this bewitching blonde. He'd been unable to think of anything but Mariah Benedict all day. He'd been so anxious to see her again that he'd left the job site early, leaving one of his men in charge to shut things down for the night. That wasn't like him. Not like him at all. But tonight he didn't feel like himself. His body was tense with an almost boyish excitement, and he felt far younger than his thirty-four years.

"Hey, I like your apartment," he commented, trying to regain his shaken composure. Somehow he knew he couldn't come on too fast or too strong with Mariah. "I've never seen one quite like it. I suppose it was once the attic?"

"Yes, I understand it was. When I was a little girl I always wanted to have a bedroom with a dormered window and a big oak tree outside of it. I don't have the oak tree here," she laughed lightly, a lilting sound that went with her blond good looks, "but I've got more than my share of dormers."

She gestured toward three small windows that faced in opposite directions. The fourth he imagined had been partitioned off for the bath. One dormer held a cheerful kitchenette while another held a flowered studio couch with matching curtains. To his relief, the apartment decor appeared to be completely feminine—there wasn't a sign of a masculine touch. And, he noted with pleasure, the place was far too small to accommodate a roommate.

As Mariah led him toward the third dormer that

26

opened onto a balcony, David let his eyes rest on the lovely contours of her tanned shoulders, bare except for tiny straps, before his gaze slipped to her small waist above her gently swaying hips. Mariah Benedict was every inch the shapely woman he had imagined was hidden under the jacket she'd worn that morning.

All afternoon his hammer had rung out her name, three beats to a nail, Ma-ri-ah . . . Ma-ri-ah . . . over and over as he'd framed in another apartment unit.

Stepping onto the tiny balcony that barely held two canvas captain chairs with a narrow wicker table between them made him acutely aware of his size. The balustraded veranda bedecked with flaming red geraniums had been constructed to accommodate a slender, lissome woman like Mariah rather than a man of his dimensions.

"Here are the tags." Mariah offered an envelope she'd taken from the table.

"Thanks." He smiled as he tucked it into a hip pocket. "I'll have to be up early to make sure they're on the plates before any of the trucks roll out of the yard in the morning. The fine for unregistered commercial vehicles is pretty steep.

"This is a great place. You even have a view," David remarked as he looked out over the tops of the trees surrounding the house. The now fading red sunset darkly crimsoned the water of the Puget Sound.

"If I stand on a chair," Mariah agreed with a laugh. "Or I suppose I would have if I were over six feet tall like you."

When he made no move to leave, Mariah asked,

27

"Would you like to sit down?" She motioned to one chair as she took the other.

"Sure." Gingerly lowering himself onto the frail-looking chair, David slowly adjusted his body, fearing the crossed supports would splinter under his weight. The last thing in the world he wanted was to sprawl in a ridiculous heap at this fascinating woman's feet.

She wanted desperately to have her question about David's marital status answered, but Mariah decided that to come right out and ask him would make her interest in him too obvious. Besides, she told herself, she had absolutely no reason to believe he found her as attractive as she did him. For all she knew he was just being polite by staying to talk for a few minutes.

After carefully settling his long-legged figure back against the canvas, and trying to relax in spite of an occasional ominous creak, David remarked, "I'm glad you're not."

"Not what?" Mariah asked with a puzzled smile.

"Not over six feet tall. I like my women short enough to tuck their heads under my chin." He stroked his hand up the muscular column of his neck, his gesture ending just below his strong jaw line.

A sudden frown creased Mariah's smooth brow as her smiling face sobered.

"What's the matter? Did I say something wrong?" He leaned toward her in the gathering dusk.

"I don't know," she answered slowly, withdrawing her gaze from his. "Somehow that sounds like a chauvinist remark, but I really can't figure out why."

"You modern women!" he chided good-naturedly. "It seems you're always looking for some macho in-

28

sult behind every innocent remark a guy makes. It's getting so I really hesitate before giving a woman a compliment. I have to consider first how she'll take it.

"Look—" starting to use the term "honey," which he'd learned the hard way really brought out the ire in feminist women, he amended, "Mariah." He reached across the distance between them and lightly laid his hand on the silken tumble of loose curls that framed her lovely face. "All I meant was that I like you exactly the way you are. Okay?"

His work-roughened fingers lightly entwined themselves in her fine-textured hair, loath to leave the lustrous fall of golden waves. His surprisingly gentle touch turned her head back so that her clear gray gaze once more met his. He'd never felt hair like hers, so clean and vibrant, yet so soft and downright enticing. He wanted to bury his face in the fragrance of her shining mane while his hands explored the curves of her desirable body. Instead, he reluctantly withdrew his hand as his better judgment took control of his senses.

"Don't you have certain things that you especially like to look at in a man?" He leaned back, resting his forearms on the wooden supports. His green eyes twinkled. "I mean, aren't there some traits that you find more attractive than others? Like preferring tanned blond men to dark-headed guys with sallow complexions? Or preferring muscled guys who work with their hands to those couch potatoes who sit on their duffs in an office all day?"

Listening to his comparisons, Mariah's lips curved into a smile in spite of herself.

"Or does every guy in pants turn you on?" he teased.

"Of course not!" Mariah protested. Her fair skin reddened at the thought of the pleasure she'd experienced just looking at David Anthony's appealing physique as she'd stood in line at the license bureau. How could she endure this increasingly intimate conversation much longer not knowing if this man was a fun-loving single or a married flirt?

"So the table turns." David laughed, his square white teeth a flash in the dark that had fallen around them. "Who's being chauvinistic now? Is there a name for female chauvinists?" he asked, expecting a flip reply.

But to his surprise, his remark failed to elicit a comment from Mariah. Unaware of the true reason behind her silence, he took her slim hand in his, afraid that he'd offended her. Touching her petal-smooth skin caused a tremor of sensuous pleasure to ripple through his body. He could hardly keep his hands off this woman! And yet if he didn't he felt certain he'd scare her away and lose any chance he had with her.

It was strange, he mused. Mariah seemed much more nervous and jumpy than he'd expected after the easy conversation she'd initiated that morning. Recalling that she had said she was tired of the cocktail scene, he decided that must be the explanation for her unexpected behavior. Obviously she was tired of guys trying to paw her. If he wasn't careful he'd end up lumped in her mind with the rest of them. An insane antagonism against the faceless men which he vividly imagined trying to get their hands on her flared within him.

"I'm only kidding." His voice was curiously husky as he released her hand. "Where would you like to go out for dinner? I owe you one. If you hadn't taken my place in line the company could be out a great deal of money right now. If I hadn't gotten back to the site when I did two truckloads of inferior two-by-fours would have been off-loaded onto the premises. No telling how many of them would have been used by my crew. The rest of the day would have been wasted ripping them all out. You deserve a steak dinner with all the trimmings."

"But you already paid me," Mariah declared.

His women. Those were the words that had disturbed her so. If this man thought that in her he'd found a little action to enjoy on the side, he had another think coming! Cool, competent. That was how she had to play this scene even though she literally trembled with conflicting emotions that alternated between hope and anger.

"And," she continued, "I think you've even given me an idea for starting my own business. So you don't owe me anything more." She forced a bright smile that almost caused her cheeks to ache.

"But we have to eat," he protested, "and I want to buy you the best steak in town. Even more than that, I want to hear all the details about your idea for a business. You say I had something to do with your thinking of it?"

She nodded mutely.

"Well then, you sure can't leave me dangling with a teaser like that."

At least if there were a little unsuspecting wife keeping the home fires burning, Mariah thought uneasily, clearly she didn't expect her handsome husband home for dinner.

You're in control here, Mariah told herself firmly.

31

Nothing's going to happen tonight that you don't permit. Although she felt an attraction to David Anthony that she couldn't deny, she didn't date married men, and she'd never made an exception to that hard-and-fast rule. Whenever she'd been approached for a date the first question she always asked was if he was married. Why couldn't she ask David Anthony the same thing? Glancing at his chiseled profile, it struck her that it seemed rude to bluntly ask this man whether or not he was single. She just couldn't understand herself. Why did she feel this way? Suddenly the answer came to her in a flash of insight. She wanted to believe that David Anthony was an honorable man—wanted to believe that he wouldn't lead her on or put her in a compromising situation. If he was the kind of person she hoped, at this point, the question would be insulting.

And truthfully, she had been anxious for him to stop by because she wanted badly to discuss her half-developed idea with him. She suspected he might have some good suggestions to help her along. This would be a business dinner, she decided, nothing more, despite the strong appeal the man held for her. But by the time the evening was over, one way or the other she would know for certain if Mr. David Anthony was unattached or taken.

"I really think I'm the one who owes you dinner," Mariah said, a sudden decisiveness straightening her supple spine. "In fact the steaks I bought with the money you paid me are marinating right now."

"If you insist," he agreed amiably. "Something sure smells good."

"Oh my gosh!" Mariah rose so quickly her leg brushed against the extended length of David Anthony's muscular calf, causing an unwanted shiver of pleasure to weaken her knees. "What you're smelling is my potatoes Romanoff casserole. It's been in the oven for hours. I've got to get it out before it's completely ruined.

"Would you mind starting the fire?" She indicated a small hibachi in the corner of the balcony. "The charcoal is already in it. It's self-lighting. Just toss in a match."

"No problem. I think I can handle that." He rose cautiously from the creaky chair.

Pausing for just a moment in the doorway to look back, watching his easy grace as David hunkered down to light the briquettes, Mariah quickly turned her face from the pleasing sight, willing her head rather than her heart to rule her actions this evening.

Her hands shook as she opened the oven door. Peering in, she saw that the casserole was all right. Maybe a little overdone and slightly dry, but passable, even though it had been on low for hours. After the elated high of the afternoon, her emotions had been simmering on low for hours too, until David Anthony's touch on her hair—a touch that went considerably beyond the casual—had suddenly sparked an ember that glowed warmly deep within her.

She could kick herself for even mentioning the steaks, she thought as she opened the refrigerator door. If she hadn't, she could have claimed the casserole was ruined and have used that as an excuse to ask him to leave. Reaching into the warm oven she added a little more sour cream to the dish.

"Smells wonderful." David's deep voice behind her startled her so that she straightened abruptly, letting the oven door shut with a bang. "I haven't had a home-cooked meal since I was home last Easter."

"Where is home?" Mariah asked, keeping her voice steady as she turned to find him only inches away. The pleasant scent of his fresh herbal aftershave and the sight of his closely shaven cheeks were proof that he'd taken pains to clean up for the evening. She longed to stroke the smooth planes of his tanned face, longed to brush the sun-bleached hair from his forehead. But wayward fancies aside, she was faced with a more realistic problem: There was no way she could put the cream carton back into the small fridge without brushing against him. And she couldn't risk that body contact. Couldn't trust her instincts not to betray her.

"It was Phoenix," he answered, moving sideways to casually rest his weight against the edge of the counter.

"Was?" Mariah asked, grateful to be able to open the refrigerator without having to touch him.

"Yes. Was. I was born and raised there but I've been up here for over ten years. I met my wife—"

Mariah's suddenly accusing gaze abruptly confronted his. He hastily amended, "Ex-wife when we were both at the University of Arizona."

"Why didn't you stay in Arizona?" Mariah forced herself to ask nonchalantly though her soaring spirits lifted the corners of her mouth into a wide smile.

"Because then I would have never met you," David teased, reaching out to circle her bare upper arms with his large warm hands.

At his gentle touch the smoldering ember within her put forth a flickering flame, quickening her pulse

34

beat and sending heated blood to race wildly through her body.

"Seriously," she urged, shrugging her arms free from his light grip.

"Seriously? Because Carla hated the climate in Arizona. She'd only gone south because her parents' marriage was in trouble and they had wanted her to get away from the stress of feeling that she was caught in the middle. She was living with her mother's sister a few blocks from campus when we met.

"When I look back on it now, I really think that all I was in Carla's life was a temporary replacement for her parents. I think any guy that had come along would have fit the bill. But then I thought I loved her and she loved me. I was willing to do anything for her. Even relocate and move up here. Anything to make her happy."

The look of pain on David's face sobered Mariah. Quietly she asked, "And was she happy?"

"At first she seemed to be. An apartment wouldn't suit her, so we bought a house with a small down payment. As long as she was shopping or buying she seemed to be thrilled with married life. She had to have the newest styles and latest models of everything you can imagine. That woman ran up bills it took me years to pay off. When my credit ran out and the plastic was worthless, she started shopping around for a new husband without telling the old one. I found out later that she'd tried out some of my friends as possibilities before the ink on our divorce decree was dry. Carla canceled our marriage agreement as callously as the stores canceled our accounts."

"Any children?" Mariah ventured to ask in a low whisper.

"No. Children are an expensive proposition, but they weren't the kind of luxury Carla had on her list." He gave a short humorless laugh.

"You never moved back to Phoenix?"

"No, I love it here. I like working with wood, building things." He respectfully rubbed his large hands along the grain of the small antique oak table that Mariah used for the extra preparation space her efficiency kitchen didn't provide.

"Don't look so sad," he gently admonished her. "Carla took me to the cleaners, but no one's going to do that to me again. Anyway, it all happened so long ago that I hardly ever think of it now." The vehement tone of his voice belied his words. "Now that I'm on the other side of the fence I can even laugh about it." But the forced chuckle that rose from his lips sounded more bitter than amused.

"There's been no one else since then?" Her voice faltered and she lowered her eyes in embarrassment.

"Nothing heavy," he assured her gently.

Once more his hands encircled her arms, this time firmly pulling her slender body closer to his rugged length. When his magnetic gaze forced her eyes back into contact with his, she watched in fascination as naked emotions played on his face. Seconds passed before the memories that clouded his eyes were dispersed by a genuine smile.

He released her. "Where are the steaks? How do you want yours? Medium? Well done?"

"Medium, please," Mariah answered, suddenly remembering how famished she was.

"A woman after my own heart," David approved as he headed out to the balcony.

Mariah rested her upper back against the refrigerator, folding her arms across her chest. The past few moments had been so emotionally charged that she needed a little time to put them into perspective, to think about everything David Anthony had revealed. She suspected that the information he had shared was a rare departure from a natural reluctance to talk about himself. The man, she would be willing to bet, was ordinarily the strong, silent type. She wondered why he'd chosen to be so open with her on such short acquaintance. The obvious answer made her heart sing with hope. Clearly the attraction she felt was not one-sided.

But, she chided herself, she had to be realistic. David Anthony might claim that his relationship with his ex-wife was over and that the wounds were healed, but despite his protests to the contrary she had seen enough pain in his eyes to realize that he'd been left with an exposed nerve. A nerve that was raw and still ached whether he chose to admit it or not.

Although she no longer had any worries about his availability, she feared he had some reservations that were going to have to be resolved before a relationship between them could develop into anything lasting or meaningful. That there was already the beginning of a relationship between them she had no doubt. His gentle touch on her hair, the way he looked at her, and the frankness with which he'd discussed his failed marriage had all convinced her of his sincere interest. The way she was stirred by the sound of his voice and the sight of him, along with the pleasurable tension that his very nearness created in her own body and heart were all unmistakable symptoms of a budding attraction that was undeniably growing stronger.

Mariah stayed in the kitchenette far longer than necessary, listening to the sound of David's melodious whistling. She didn't want to be alone with him in the quiet, dark atmosphere of the balcony just yet. She needed a little time to get her emotions under control and her mind back on track.

Fussing over the individual salads she took from the refrigerator vividly brought back the excitement she'd felt earlier in the afternoon while preparing them. The sight of the crisp green lettuce, the dark red julienned beets, and the marinated artichoke hearts brought back the time when her hands had been occupied with the mundane task of preparing the vegetables, freeing her mind to run a mile a minute as it conceived and elaborated on a new idea for a business. She could hardly wait to see how David Anthony, who she was convinced was a very practical man, would react to her scheme.

CHAPTER THREE

With the meal over, the dishes stacked in the sink, and the charcoal reduced to a gray pile of ashes, Mariah and David sat together on the queen-sized convertible couch that served a dual purpose in the small apartment. His arm rested on the top of the couch behind her head, but he carefully resisted the strong impulse he felt to put his arm around her and pull her tightly against him. Go slow, he reminded himself. When it came to business deals he'd learned long ago that restraint and patience could eventually pay off in huge dividends. It was easy to keep that in mind when dealing in terms of building lots, bank loans, and negative or positive cash flow, but much more difficult to apply the principle to his future with the lovely woman sitting so close.

"The steaks were perfect," Mariah murmured contentedly.

"The potatoes were fabulous," David added appreciatively, unable to resist lifting her slender wrist to his lips and gently kissing its silken inner side. To his delight she didn't shy away, but rewarded him with a bright smile as her slim body moved almost imperceptibly closer to his.

Although she'd forgotten to buy wine to serve with

the meal, Mariah felt a warm glow suffuse her entire being. David's touch, his very nearness, generated a heat in her senses far more intense than the costliest wine could ever induce. She longed to feel his warm, moist lips that had so gently caressed her wrist claim her mouth, but she suspected she would have to wait for that moment. David Anthony was far too much the gentleman to kiss her without having asked her for a real date. She knew instinctively that this impromptu evening spent together wouldn't count as a date in his mind.

It had been wonderful having a man at her kitchen table. There hadn't been an awkward moment between them from the time he brought the grilled steaks to the table and pulled out her chair for her before seating himself. During the meal they'd enjoyed an easy rapport that she found remarkable considering how terribly attracted she was to him. She'd been afraid that she might not be able to eat a bite, but fortunately in the war between her clamoring stomach and her singing senses, her stomach had won out. She hadn't inhibited David's hunger either, she remembered with a grin. He'd eaten nearly the entire casserole, though she had to admit she'd had her fair share. They'd both been famished, and when they were done not a trace of the two large steaks had been left on either of their plates.

Although Mariah had been anxious to talk over her plan for a business, seeing how hungry he was, she had decided to wait until she didn't have to share his attention with his meal.

When David had learned that the potato casserole was one of her mother's specialties, he'd insisted on hearing about her unremarkable childhood spent growing up in Tacoma, a city somewhat smaller than Seattle. He'd matched her reminiscences with amusing recollections of his own coming of age until Mariah was beginning to feel as though she'd known him for a long time. In fact, she couldn't remember when she'd felt so comfortable and at ease with a man. It was a relief to be with someone who was interested in talking to her and who could hold up his end of the conversation. Most of the men she'd met in her adult life had been either so limited in their interests and education that they were positively dull, or frankly only interested in her body. Or worse yet, both. But even though they had spent such a short time together, Mariah knew that David Anthony was a different sort altogether.

"In less than six hours I have to be on the job again," he groaned. Stifling a yawn he pulled a blue floral pillow from behind his back.

"In the middle of the night?" Mariah asked incredulously.

"It may be the middle of the night to you, but I'll be hard at work as soon as that sun starts to come up over the horizon." David smiled, picturing her as she must look at that time of the morning, deeply asleep, her cheeks flushed with a rosy glow, her tousled curls a soft golden frame around her lovely head, only the sheerest of fabric covering the secrets of her gorgeous body. "In this kind of weather we work from sunup to sundown, seven days a week. We need all the daylight hours we can get."

"That's awful! How can your boss get anyone to work for him? *He* must *really* be a slave driver!" Mariah exclaimed.

David laughed, a bold sound that sent tingles of

pleasure running through Mariah's body. "I suppose some of the men might agree with you. The boss is demanding and he's a perfectionist, I'll grant you that. He won't put up with shoddy materials or shoddy workmanship. But he's a fair man and he pays well and even more importantly he keeps his crews working. Don't be too hard on him. Remember, you have to give even the devil his due, and the men can see that he demands even more out of himself than he does out of them."

"But why would anyone want to work that hard?" Mariah asked.

"Money. You see, honey," David slipped the endearment in, pleased to see that it didn't cause as much as a blink of her lovely eyelids, "building is a business that depends on the elements. We have to work while the weather is good. People in our trade have to be a little like squirrels, I guess. We work all the overtime we can get in the summer, socking away our 'acorns' in the bank to tide us over during the wet season. We get our time off when the weather is bad."

"That can't be very enjoyable."

"Oh, I wouldn't say that. Just remember that when it's wet and rainy here, the sun is shining in Hawaii."

"Is that what you do in the winter?" Mariah asked. "Do you spend it in Hawaii, soaking up the sun?"

"Not exactly." David evaded a direct answer. "I haven't made it there yet, but I plan to real soon. So far I've managed to keep busy right here."

Mariah felt a twinge of uneasiness. She shouldn't have asked him that. He had told her how deeply in debt his wife had left him. He probably had to spend his winters working a second job just to dig himself

42

out of that hole and get back on his feet. Silently she resolved to be more careful in the future about not reminding him of his past.

"The summers are grueling," he admitted, "but I enjoy what I'm doing so much that I usually don't mind the long hours and the exhaustion. But tonight is an exception. I'd like to be bright-eyed and bushy-tailed, but the truth is that I'm beat. Would you mind if I put this pillow on your lap and stretched out? I want to hear all about your idea for a business. Trust me. I think better lying down."

Without waiting for an answer he ceremoniously settled the pillow on her lap and laid his head upon it, swinging his legs up and letting his feet dangle over the end of the long couch. Looking down into his face Mariah had to resist the almost overwhelming impulse to cuddle his head against her breast.

"Now, let's go over this plan of yours," he said. He was anxious to find out how this bewitching woman's mind worked. For that matter, to find out just what she had in mind!

When he reached for her hand and held it on his chest Mariah could feel the strong thudding of his heart. Her awareness of David's vitality was so overpowering that she found it difficult to concentrate. But seeing the genuine interest in his eyes, she managed to collect her wandering thoughts.

"It caught me off guard this morning when you suggested that I buy your tags, especially when you offered to pay me for doing it. But I was even more surprised when other people asked me to do the same thing."

"I'm not," David interjected matter-of-factly. "It was a good idea, and I wasn't the only one who

43

thought so. So what does that have to do with your plan?"

"Well," Mariah said a little tentatively, feeling a shy reluctance to throw her idea out to his probing scrutiny. "I've never made eighty dollars so quickly or easily in my entire life. It occurred to me that I might be able to make a business out of standing in lines. I'm sure there were several other people in that room who would have paid me to get their tags for them if they'd known what I was doing. What do you think?"

"You're probably right," David agreed. "But you couldn't count on that being the case every day. And not only that," he abruptly raised himself on an elbow as an appalling thought occurred to him, "the jail is right there in the county-city building. There are cops all over that place. Sooner or later if you were seen hanging around there propositioning people with your suggestion, someone would be sure to get the wrong idea. I don't want to have to bail you out of a cellful of hookers!"

Mariah laughed and gently pushed his solid shoulder back down. "That's not part of the plan. Believe me, I have no intention of getting arrested. I've never even had a traffic ticket. A couple of warnings on the freeway," she admitted, "but that's all."

"I'm not surprised," David said with a wry grin. "I can just picture a trooper pulling you over and finding himself completely disarmed by those wide eyes of yours. You'd probably have to be going down the wrong side of the freeway to actually get a ticket. But a guy like me, five miles over the speed limit and I get it in the neck."

"Poor baby," Mariah purred, glad of the excuse

44

he'd given her to gently stroke his throat, though she stopped just short of the springy blond hair that curled enticingly in the open neck of his shirt. "Your neck seems just fine to me. You know, some of the troopers are women now. Maybe you'll get lucky the next time you're caught speeding and get one of them. I'm sure she'd give you a break." And her phone number, Mariah added silently.

David snorted. "Never happen. I always get those young male hotshots who're out to get their quota. But all kidding aside, I do think that hanging around the county-city building could be a problem for a woman who looks like you."

"That's not what I had in mind," Mariah assured him, recognizing that he had a point. "There are all sorts of other things I could do."

"Such as?" He quizzically raised a blond brow.

"Such as gassing up cars for people who want to get an early start on the weekend. I could pay traffic tickets, return items to stores—things like that."

"I'm beginning to get the picture," David said. "You might have something here. Hey, come to think of it, I've got a couple of ideas for you. A lot of the guys who work for the company are from other places and live in motels during the peak season. They bring their VCRs along with them because there's not much on TV by the time they get off. They like to watch a video while they wind down at night. But the problem is that the video stores aren't open the right hours. Those guys really need someone who would pick up and return the movies for them." He shook his head in disbelief. "Some of those guys are such procrastinators that the video stores even call our office about bringing the tapes back.

I've seen guys end up paying as much as twenty bucks for a movie that was supposed to cost them ninety-nine cents!"

"That sounds so far-fetched I can hardly believe it," Mariah said, thinking of what she could have done with that wasted money. "Are you serious?"

"Absolutely." David nodded. "And my second thought was that the company could use someone like you to get all the permits it takes to keep us in operation. I've wasted more than one day waiting to get a set of plans approved down at City Hall. I'm sure the boss would rather pay you to wait for them than have me over there pacing the floor."

"So you like the idea?" Mariah asked.

"It has a lot of possibilities," David agreed.

"If I were to advertise," Mariah said enthusiastically, "I bet there are a lot of people who would use my services. The lady standing behind me at the license bureau today said that if she'd known I would buy her tags for her she could have eaten her lunch instead of wasting her time in line."

"Do you have enough money for an advertising campaign?"

She grimaced. "I don't even have next month's rent payment! How much do you think I'd need?"

"At least a thousand," David remarked, thinking of the enormous expense he had incurred when he'd started his contracting business. "Maybe closer to two if you really want to do it right. Your idea is so unique that you'll probably have to run a few radio spots on the local stations to get it off the ground. You'll need a morning spot and a late-afternoon time. Catch the commuters—the people stuck in traffic who've been putting off doing the things you're offer-

46

ing to do for them. Lay on a real guilt trip. Make them glad to hire you to get those nagging little jobs off their backs."

"Two thousand? Then the whole idea is out!" Mariah wailed dejectedly.

"Now calm down." David patted her hand in a soothing manner. "There are small business loans designed just for people like you. I have a good friend at the bank the company uses for most of its business. We went to school together. I'll get in touch with him right away. But first you have to be realistic about how much money you'll need.

"First of all, you'll need a business phone. If I'm not mistaken, you just have time to make it into this year's Yellow Pages. And you'll have to have an answering service."

"How much does an answering machine cost? A cheap model—" Mariah amended her question, feeling more hopeless by the minute.

"Not a machine," he corrected, "a real service. People don't like to leave messages on a machine. They usually do it only if they're really desperate. They'd hang up before they even listened to your recorded message. They'd want to talk to a person and be reassured that you'll call back. That's the benefit of employing people who are trained to keep the caller on the line."

"I suppose you're right. I know I usually hang up myself. I hate those things beeping in my ear."

"You will need a beeper," he continued, "so that the answering service will be able to get in touch with you wherever you are.

"And you're going to need a PC to keep track of your calls, your clients and your appointments."

47

"A PC? What's that? David, be reasonable," Mariah pleaded. "How can I need things when I don't even know what they are?"

"A PC is a personal computer. You'll want to keep all your records on discs. That way you won't need an office or an accountant."

"But I don't know the first thing about computers!" Mariah moaned, "or accounting either, for that matter. I'd have to go to school to learn how to use the computer and keep my accounts."

"No," David lightly dismissed her concern. "It sounds a lot more complicated than it is. You can buy programs for the accounting. All you have to be able to do is type in the data. I can teach you what you'd need to know right away. After that you can take instruction from the store you buy the computer from.

"And what about your car? Is it reliable? Low on gas mileage? You don't want all your profits going into repairs and fuel."

Mariah shook her head, feeling totally dejected. "My car has had it. Each time I turn the key it takes longer and longer to cough to life. My battery is shot. Probably won't even hold another quick charge. And my tires are as smooth as the pavement. It seems like the gas runs through it as fast as I pump it in."

"Then you're going to have to lease a new one. It's best that way anyhow," he patiently explained, "because then you can write your car expenses off against your business.

"You need a catchy name for your business and you'll need a graphic artist to design an original logo for your cards and stationery."

"I hadn't thought of any of those things." The misery she felt at knowing that her idea was totally impractical was replaced momentarily by surprise at the depth of his knowledge. "How come you know so much about starting a business? Did you ever start one before?"

"I've just been around a few people who have."

David chose to answer Mariah's first question, but to ignore the second. Marrying a woman as mercenary as Carla had made him overly cautious. He'd been working for someone else during their marriage and his income had been modest. Even so, she'd managed to run up bills that had taken him over two years to pay off. He supposed she'd really done him a favor. Once out from under Carla's debts, he'd struck out on his own, determined to make a bundle, as much to show her what she'd lost as to prove to himself he could do it. The only problem was he'd had to deal with a few fortune hunters along the way. He had no use for a woman who was after his money, and he preferred to let this one go on thinking he was a day laborer. It was too soon to let Mariah know that Superior Construction Company and David Anthony were one and the same.

His explanation seemed to satisfy her, for she commented, "And I thought it would be so simple. Just go out and stand in line like I did this morning. I'm really naïve. No, not naïve, just plain stupid. I guess I did think I could put a little ad in the classifieds, and when things were slow, that I could hang around the county-city building picking up customers like I did this morning."

"Mariah, I don't want to sound crude or insulting because believe me, I don't mean it that way," David said with all the sincerity he could muster, "but

49

whether you realize it or not, you picked up more than a few customers."

Caught up in her dejected thoughts, Mariah questioned, "What are you talking about?"

"Me," he said finally after a long moment spent searching her clear gray eyes and finding only innocence there.

"But it was your idea to come here after work to get your tags," she protested, a hot flush spreading across her fair face.

"And it was a great idea!" he hastened to add. "But I don't think I want you standing in any more lines if this is what's going to happen."

"I've been standing in lines all my life from kindergarten on and nothing like this has ever happened to me before." Indignation flared within her.

"You don't think I believe that for a minute, do you?" he asked.

His scowl was so earnest that it struck her as comical. Feeling her momentary annoyance fade away as quickly as it had come, she couldn't resist teasing. "Well, there was that sailor at the bus depot—he was really cute in those bell bottoms. And there is a guy at the employment office who picks up his check on the same day I do. Intriguing tattoos," she mused, a grin lighting her eyes. "And come to think of it, just last week at the supermarket a good-looking guy with a basket loaded with food asked me if I wanted to come home with him and help him cook."

"And?"

"And what?"

"Did you?"

Suddenly his questions weren't funny anymore and she wasn't amused. "Do I look that easy? Is that why you came up here tonight?" Mariah stiffened under the weight of David's head. Pulling her hand from his, she pushed at the pillow on her lap.

"Wait a minute," David protested, grabbing the pillow with both hands, struggling against her efforts to dislodge him. "Wait just a minute. What you look is absolutely gorgeous and not the least bit 'easy,' as you call it. I happened to be looking toward the door when you came into the licensing bureau. From the corner of my eye I watched you standing there trying to decide which line to join. I literally held my breath, hoping it would be the one I was in. Then, while you stood behind me, your perfume nearly drove me crazy. I wanted to talk to you, but I couldn't think of the right thing to say for an opener."

"It sure took you a long time to think!" she exclaimed, feeling more than a little placated. "I looked at your back for nearly thirty minutes."

"Remember," he teased, "I thought I still had forty minutes left. I was mentally trying out every scenario I could imagine. I tried to think what Bobby Ewing would do if he were in my shoes, but I only drew a blank. I even hoped there'd be a disaster so I could shield you with my body! I was envisioning that scene when you asked me how long I thought we were going to stand there. You're lucky I hadn't grabbed you before then and bellowed 'earthquake!' "

"You're a nut," Mariah said, her good humor completely restored. "Are you sure it's safe for me to be alone with you like this?"

"I don't know," David answered with a devilish grin. "That's something you'll have to decide for yourself. But seriously, I'd like to know why a woman who's as desirable as you are is still single and unattached?"

"I don't get a chance to meet many men." Mariah's tone was pensive.

"You must be joking. In a cocktail lounge? I'd think you'd meet more men there than anywhere else."

"Do you spend a lot of time in one?" she asked pointedly.

"Me?"

"Yes, you," she pressed, sure of his answer.

"Of course not! I'm a busy guy. I've got better things to do with my time."

"See? You answered your own question. Most of the decent men who go to such places are with their wives or dates. The other ones who spend their nights on a bar stool aren't the kind who turn me on. Besides, I blew a whole month's worth of tips on the biggest flashiest set of zirconiums I could find to weight down the third finger of my left hand. Between the two-carat solitaire and the row of half-carat stones in the phony wedding band, most guys got the message that I wasn't available. The only type that didn't take the hint were the lechers who were out determined to cheat on their wives. But one drink 'accidentally' spilled in their laps usually took care of them." She giggled in spite of herself.

"But there must have been someone," David persisted, taking her hand again and holding it gently in both of his.

"There was," Mariah admitted. "It was one of those unrealistic high school romances. We were going to be married when he finished college. But by the time he'd completed two degrees we didn't seem to have much in common. It hurt for a while, but not

52

as badly as I expected. The trouble was, by that time most of the friends we'd had were married and there weren't many single guys around anymore."

"No one since then?"

"As you put it, nothing heavy."

"Speaking of that, am I too heavy on your lap?"

"Not at all." Mariah laughed, glad to have the conversation shifted so easily.

"Now that we have all that cleared up, let's talk some more about your business."

"I'm afraid it was just wishful thinking," Mariah put in quickly. "I don't know a thing about half of what you were talking about, and I certainly don't have any extra money. Nor do I know anyone who has who would be willing to help me get started. I'm afraid I'll just have to forget about it. But it did seem like a good idea all afternoon."

"It is a good idea," David insisted. "It's a terrific idea. And if you're even half the woman I think you are, you're going to pull it off."

"You really think I can do it?" Mariah asked.

"I know you can do it. How about it?"

"If you think I can, and you're willing to give me advice, I'll give it a try. After all, what have I got to lose? If I go bankrupt can I still draw unemployment?" she joked.

"I wouldn't worry about that if I were you." He squeezed her hand reassuringly, delighted at this evidence of her spunk. She would make a go of it, he resolved. He'd make damn sure of it. "Actually, the amount of money you'll need is small compared to most other beginning businesses. You don't need to rent a building, you don't need to hire any personnel, you don't need to buy an inventory of goods or materials—"

She cut him off. "But according to your calculations I'll need several thousand dollars just to get started."

"Don't worry about it. It can be handled. Look, I'll call Jeff Holden at my bank during my morning break. We played football together in college. You get some stuff written down on paper and go in to talk with him. See what he says."

"I will need a car," she thought aloud.

"You can lease a small compact. The morning paper should have a lot of ads in it. They'll give you an idea about how much that will cost."

"I'll call about a phone and check the prices on computers."

"Remember to call a printer about cards and flyers."

"I'll need a name for the business. Maybe something with procrastinators in it?"

"Nope. Too long. Use that word for humor in your ads."

"How much does a radio spot cost?"

"Call a station tomorrow and ask for a salesman. Look in the Yellow Pages for the number." David closed his eyes as his answers became shorter.

"I can stand in line for people at concerts," Mariah mused aloud. "In fact, I could hold a place for a lot of people at the same time. It would be well worth my time then."

"Mm-hmm," David agreed.

"I could pick up tickets at the airport, or at ticket offices . . ."

"Mm-hmm." His breathing was becoming more regular and deep.

"I could dump you right onto the floor," Mariah continued in the same tone of voice, smiling down into his relaxed, sundarkened face.

"Mm-hmm," came the sleepy reply.

"You aren't listening to a word I say, are you?" she asked quietly.

"Mmmm," he answered, the sound a purr in his throat as he burrowed his head deeper into the pillow.

"You are sound asleep, aren't you?" she asked. Then, getting no response, she finally allowed the fingers of her free hand to indulge themselves by gently pushing back the sun-bleached shock of hair that brushed across his high forehead.

For a long while she sat still, holding the pillow with his sleeping head upon it, stroking his hair, tracing the lines of his brows and the straight plane of his nose with her finger, her mind teeming with the ideas he'd suggested. The more she thought, the more excited she became at the prospect of starting her own business.

At last, anxious to get her ideas on paper, she leaned her face close to his and pressed her lips against the firm warm flesh of his forehead. Then she left two fluttery kisses on his eyelids. She hesitated over his sensuous lips but thoughtfully drew back. When her lips touched his, she decided, she wanted it to be with a mutual pleasure, an expression of passion, a celebration of the attraction they felt for one another. The thought caused a delicious shiver of anticipation to surge through her.

Slowly she extricated herself from beneath the pillow and checked to see that his head was still resting in a comfortable position. Then, opening the painted chest she used as a coffee table and which held her bedding, she took out a soft down quilt and laid it over his sleeping form.

Sitting at her small kitchen table, Mariah made list after list. Consulting the evening paper she noticed ads that she had been totally unaware of just hours before. Engrossed as she was, every slight movement of the sleeping man on her couch drew her attention. No matter if her scheme didn't get off the ground, she'd met David Anthony and that was really all that mattered. Dreamily she envisioned long winter evenings, when the weather was bad, spent with him at her side.

CHAPTER FOUR

After making a futile circle of the parking lot, Mariah desperately inched her car into the only available spot. A spot designed for fuel-efficient compacts rather than her old full-sized model, she thought with dismay as she squeezed her slender body out of the narrow space between the thick door and the car's frame. Fearful that she'd lose her nerve if she allowed her mind to dwell on the cost of replacing the old hulk of a car, she resolutely quickened her steps. As she hurried across the sun-heated tarmac she glanced up at the sign board. It was 10:27.

Watching the digital display change from time to temperature, she saw it was already eighty-eight degrees even though it was only midmorning. It was going to be a scorcher. Thinking of David working from sunup to sundown in the heat of the day, Mariah decided that it would be unreasonable to expect him to take her out that evening even though she was sure he'd keep his promise if she held him to it. But she'd make other plans. Plans she was sure a hungry, tired man would readily approve. She'd pick up some cold cuts and a six-pack of beer at the deli and have them waiting when he arrived.

The sudden cool air inside the bank struck her bare

shoulders and arms with unpleasant needling prickles, causing her to shiver convulsively. Was this an omen? she wondered, fighting down a silly urge to flee. Would her application be turned down? Telling herself to behave like the responsible businesswoman she hoped to be, she hastily crossed over to the receptionist's desk.

"I have an appointment with Mr. Holden. I'm Mariah Benedict," she informed the primly dressed woman.

"I'll tell Mr. Holden you're here." The woman spoke coolly, pointedly taking in Mariah's strapless black sundress with a disapproving glance. "Please be seated." She indicated a group of couches near a clump of potted trees.

As Mariah walked across the carpeted floor, the chilled stares of the other bank clerks almost seemed to penetrate her exposed flesh. From the time she'd stepped into the bank, she'd become aware that she was inappropriately dressed, had known that she was so uneasy because she didn't look the part she hoped to play.

How could she have chosen the simple sundress that was held to her body merely by a piece of elastic gathered above her bust and another at her waist? Why hadn't she worn a jacket and skirt like the women who surrounded her? She groaned inwardly, wishing the sofa would swallow her up. No wonder the air-conditioning was turned on so high. That was the only way anyone professionally dressed in a suit could stand to work in the building on the blistering summer day. That she had blundered was all too apparent. But that thought hadn't occurred to her when, after her hasty shower, the black dress had seemed to be the only thing she could slip into quickly enough to get to the bank on time.

The shrill persistent ring of the phone had abruptly awakened her from a deep sleep only an hour before. She'd been disoriented, surprised to find herself on the couch with the quilt she remembered having covered David Anthony with tucked solicitously around her. Evidently she'd fallen asleep at the kitchen table after spending hours compiling list after list of the items she would need to start her business.

"Hi," David's unmistakable voice had answered her groggy greeting.

"I just called Jeff at the bank and he has a 10:30 cancellation. Can you make it?"

A quick glance at her watch had thrown her into near panic. But after kicking off the too-warm covering and sitting up, she'd answered levelly, "Of course I'll make it," carefully concealing her distress at being in such a wrinkled, disarrayed state. After David had gone to so much trouble for her, she hadn't been able to tell him that his arrangements wouldn't be all right.

"Are you sure?" He had seemed dubious. "You sound pretty sleepy to me and I know it's short notice. Why don't I call Jeff back to see if he has something later, or even tomorrow?"

"Oh no, David, don't do that," she had protested. "I'm anxious to get started. I really appreciate you doing this for me."

"No problem. Did you read my note?"

"What note?"

"The one I left on the kitchen table. You're not off the couch yet, are you?"

"I don't even remember how I got here."

"I do," David's voice had taken on a peculiar husky note. "I couldn't believe it when I woke up and found you sound asleep with your beautiful face resting in a scattered pile of papers. When I conked out on you last night, you should have kicked me out. With me sprawled all over your couch you didn't have anywhere to sleep.

"When I carried you to the sofa you didn't even stir. But believe me," he'd teased, "it took all my willpower to keep from ravishing your unconscious body."

"David!" She'd reddened, embarrassed but not unpleasantly so. "Where are you calling from? Can anyone hear you?"

He'd chuckled, amused at her reaction. "Not a soul. I'm on my morning break. Calling from a outside booth. Another guy is waiting to use the phone but he's out of earshot. I'm anxious to hear over dinner tonight how you make out with the loanshark."

"Is he that bad?" She was wide awake by that time and beginning to realize the significance of the meeting David had arranged with the banker.

"No. I'm just kidding. Don't let him come on to you too strong though. If he tries anything remind him that you're there for business only."

"Now you're really worrying me. What's he like?"

"You'll have to decide for yourself." David's cryptic answer had puzzled her. "And if we keep on talking you'll miss your appointment for sure. I wrote the bank's address on the note I left you."

After hanging up she'd found his note lying on top of the pile of lists she'd made. She'd smiled as she'd read his bold script:

Good Morning, Sleeping Beauty,

When you read this I will be long gone—off to work for the slave driver. I'll call you before ten to let you know what I find out from Jeff. See you tonight for dinner—this time my treat. I'm rooting for you, David.

Beneath his signature was the address of the bank, which she'd noted was halfway across town. It had almost seemed impossible that she could make it at all.

And that was why, she rationalized, she had pulled on her sundress over her still-damp body, slipped on a pair of bikini underpants, stepped into her sandals, grabbed her lists from the kitchen table and dashed out the door. She casually put her hand to her hair, finding it still slightly wet. Fortunately the breeze from her open car windows and the heat of the summer day had helped dry it a bit.

If only she'd taken a minute to grab her white jacket she would have felt more respectable. As a cocktail waitress she'd been required to wear a lot of skimpy outfits, but no matter how ridiculous they'd been, she'd never felt more underdressed than she did now bearing the frosty stares of the women working at desks nearby. Much more of this and her already undermined confidence would be completely shaken.

"Ms. Benedict?" a suave male voice inquired from behind her.

"Yes," Mariah said as she jumped up from the couch, clumsily dropping her pocketbook to the floor.

Stooping to retrieve it, she looked up the length of

knife-creased gabardine slacks, partially covered by a smartly cut linen sport jacket. Its opening revealed an immaculate white shirt accented by a faultlessly knotted striped tie. Straightening quickly to a standing position she found herself face to face with an impeccably groomed man. Perfectly layered, stylishly cut hair, a closely shaven tanned face, straight white teeth and clear blue eyes left her with the impression that she was in the company of someone who'd just stepped out of the pages of a prominent business magazine's profile of Men on the Move.

"I'm Jeff Holden." He extended a hand which Mariah was quick to note was as fastidiously cared for as the rest of him.

"Mariah Benedict," she said, shifting her handbag awkwardly to her left hand in order to place her right hand in his, wondering what ruggedly handsome David Anthony and this man ever found in common.

"Come into my office," he said, lightly touching her bare elbow to guide her toward an open door.

"I thought you said he was a friend of yours!" Mariah wailed tearfully, her words muffled against David Anthony's sweat dampened T-shirt.

After leaving the bank she'd let the hot tears that had threatened to overcome her composure flow freely. In her entire life she had never suffered through an experience more humiliating than the interview she'd had with Jeff Holden. That he'd flatly refused her the loan wasn't wholly the reason for her extreme agitation. Almost more disturbing was the belittling way he'd done it.

Using the back of her hand to wipe away the flow of stinging tears, she'd blindly headed her car for

David's work site. Fortunately he'd told her the location over dinner the night before or she didn't know what she would have done. She needed David, and right then no one else would do.

Once there it hadn't been difficult to spot his tall muscular shape among a group of men busily engaged in hammering up wall supports for the huge complex. She'd driven her car as close as possible before abandoning it to run across the lumber-strewn ground, seeking the comfort of David's arms, the solace of his words.

Seeing her coming, David had jumped nimbly to the ground, stripping off his heavy leather work gloves as he'd strode rapidly to meet her.

Distraught, heedless of the interested stares of the other members of the crew, Mariah had wrapped her arms around David's muscular chest, clinging to him in her humiliation.

"Here, just a minute. Let me take this off." David gently straightened up her wilted form, then quickly unbuckled his tool belt before dropping it to the ground. "Now, come here, honey, and tell me all about it." His arms enveloped her shaking frame, pulling her close as his hands comfortingly caressed her bare upper back.

"I've never been so humiliated in all my life."

"By whom? Jeff?"

"I thought you said he was a football player," Mariah said accusingly, pulling back from his embrace in order to confront him.

"He was," David answered quizzically. "He was a running end. What's that got to do with anything?"

"He either ran in the other direction when he saw

63

the opposing team coming or he's had a lot of plastic surgery since then," Mariah said sarcastically.

"He's a snake! Pure and simple! A snake!" She managed to get the accusation out before she resumed her sobbing.

"Now calm down," David soothed, secretly unsure whether he was angry at Jeff for upsetting Mariah or pleased that she couldn't stand his old best friend and sometimes rival. Drawing her back into his arms, he decided it was the latter. Knowing that Mariah was one woman who wasn't taken in by Jeff's urbane charm only endeared her to him more.

"I don't know how he can be your friend. I can't imagine him with a hair out of place, or doing an honest day's work."

"He has changed quite a lot since our college days. I take it you didn't get the loan," David observed dryly. "But what did he say to get you so riled up?"

"He said that he wouldn't loan any of the bank's precious money for such a harebrained idea to a cocktail waitress whose business experience was limited to making petty change from her drink tray!" The disjointed sentence came out in one rush of breath.

"He said that?" David asked.

"Well, not in those exact words," Mariah admitted grudgingly, "but that's exactly what he meant!"

"Have you got a tissue in your purse?" David asked after ineffectively trying to wipe the streaming tears from her face with his fingers.

"Yes," she answered, turning in his arms to fumble unsuccessfully with the flap of her shoulder bag.

"Give me that." Taking her bag, he rummaged

around until he found a small pink package. Removing a facial tissue he tenderly dried her tears.

Under the close scrutiny of David's green eyes, Mariah felt her humiliating anger dissolve, leaving only a weak melting feeling in its place as her heart began to thump erratically. Her only thoughts were of David, his face so close to hers that a mere inch separated his mouth from her pulsing lips.

Feeling an uncustomary lightheadedness, David pulled his hardhat off and tossed it down to join his toolbelt. It was hot, damned hot, but he knew the sun's rays weren't responsible for heating the blood that was madly racing through his veins. The small woman who stood before him, defenses down, all wide eyes and seductively pouting lips, was having an effect on him as unnerving as heatstroke. Taking her almost roughly by the arm, he led her a few paces to the opposite side of the construction shed, out of sight of the crew, grateful that he had enough sense left to want to shelter their inevitable kiss from curious eyes. Once they'd reached the far side of the shed, he took her back into his arms.

"David, I should never have come here," Mariah protested weakly. "I've been on my own since I was eighteen years old. I don't go running to cry on someone's shoulder whenever I'm disappointed about something. I don't know what's the matter with me; I should have never bothered you at work. I'm used to standing on my own two feet. And that's what I should have done today." She straightened her shoulders and sniffed.

Gazing down at her, caught by her beauty, he barely heard her words. When a puzzled expression crossed her face he let out an involuntary groan. She

65

couldn't know the devastating effect she was having on him. Couldn't know that the sight of the wet tears clinging like crystal drops to her long lashes, the sweet caress of her heated breath upon his cheek, and the agitated heaving of her firm breasts against his chest were intoxicating him, drugging his senses. All that existed for him was the touch of her curves against his heated length, the sight of her beautiful face so pleadingly close to his, the heady smell of her perfume filling his senses with a desire so compelling he had no choice other than to yield to its demand.

An irresistible force drew his lips closer to hers as the blood that was now like liquid fire raced through his veins. He'd meant the kiss to be light, a short sip of the stimulating delight he'd imagined her provocative mouth would hold. But once he captured her lips with his, his will weakened and his senses reigned.

His mouth covered the gentle softness of hers, demanding, even daring to force a response. When her lips tentatively parted, his questing tongue was quick to press the advantage, invading the moist recesses of her sweet mouth. Feeling her arms reach up to encircle his neck and her tongue seek his, he responded passionately to her wordless invitation.

The kiss deepened in intensity, its captivating power creating an urgent need within him. No longer aware of conscious thought, he was absorbed in sensation. Only the feel of Mariah's luscious body arched tightly against his, her tantalizing smooth skin beneath his sensitized fingertips, and the silken fall of her golden hair softly grazing his forearms consumed his stunned senses.

"Whoo-ee! Excuse *me!*"

Recognizing his foreman's voice, the drawled raucous cheer jolted David back to reality. Loosening his hold on Mariah he looked up to see the man gleefully grinning as he pulled an armful of two-by-fours from the pile next to the shed.

"Don't let me bother you, Dave. Go right ahead. I won't look," the man teased with an exaggerated wink as he shouldered his load and started to walk away.

Mariah jerked herself from David's arms, stepping back away from him. Suddenly her voice rang out, "Ouch!"

"What's the matter?"

"I think I stepped on a nail." Gingerly trying to put her weight on her injured foot, Mariah felt a sharp stab of pain.

"Let me see," David ordered, his voice filled with concern.

"It'll be all right," Mariah insisted. "I don't think it went in very far. I'm sure I can walk on it." She limped a few steps.

"So much for your standing on your own two feet!" Effortlessly swooping her up into his arms, David strode toward his truck. After opening the door he deposited her on the high seat and in one swift motion removed her thin-soled shoe.

A tiny red pinprick showed against the white of her high instep. Squeezing the wound produced a small drop of blood.

"That hurts more than the nail did," Mariah protested, trying to withdraw her foot. "What are you doing?"

"This's the best way to cleanse a puncture," David explained, holding tightly to her slim foot and

67

squeezing out a little more blood. "How long has it been since you had a tetanus shot?"

"About six months. A drunk lurched into me when I was carrying a tray full of drinks. I cut my hand picking up the glass."

"Then it will still be effective," he said, continuing to minister to her wound.

He liked the way her foot with its crimson painted nails fitted snugly into the palm of his large hand. He wanted to run his free hand around her enticingly slim ankle and over her tanned leg to feel the swell of her shapely calf. As if reading his mind, Mariah tugged her foot from his grasp.

"I'm going to take you home," he announced.

"But my car—" Mariah started to protest.

"No 'buts' about it. Give me your keys."

"I left them in the ignition, I think," Mariah said as she started to rummage around in her bag again.

"I'll get another guy to bring your car around after work. We've got to disinfect that wound. Besides, you haven't told me what really happened at the bank."

He knew that her foot was not badly injured. Using it as an excuse to be alone with her was pretty flimsy, especially with the amount of work there was to be done on the site. But he wanted to kiss her again. He wanted to hold her tightly against his yearning body and feel the thrill of her sensuous lips against his once more.

After he'd shut the door on the passenger side of the truck, Mariah watched as David strode toward the platform where his group of men worked. The effortless way they lifted the heavy boards and swung their hammers seemed like a synchronized dance, one she would have enjoyed watching, appreciating their male grace if she weren't so acutely aware of the maleness of their foreman. But his particular elegance of motion captured her full attention, leaving the impression of the others as background characters supporting his lead role.

He spoke a few words to the men, then as he turned back toward her, her rapidly beating heart lurched. Her fingers raised to her tingling lips as her gaze followed his movements. Not missing a stride, he first scooped up his gloves, then his hat, and finally his tool belt. Coming closer to the truck, his face broke into a smile. Instantly she felt her own answering smile beneath her fingertips.

With a thud, his equipment landed in the back of the pickup before he took the driver's seat beside her.

"Don't you have to tell your boss where you're going?" Mariah asked.

"I won't worry about that if you don't." David shot her a rakish smile as he swung the battered truck over the bumpy dirt road leading out of the construction site.

CHAPTER FIVE

Sitting beside David in the cab, Mariah could feel an electric tension mounting between her and the man who seemed to be totally involved with skillfully weaving the pickup in and out among the slower-moving vehicles on the six-lane freeway. Attempts at conversation had been futile because the roar of the air coming through the open windows combined with racket from the noisy engine was almost deafening at the speed he was driving. But she didn't mind the pregnant silence that hung between them. She needed time to think, time to observe, time to feel.

With her body still singing from David's ardent embrace, she couldn't keep her gaze from lingering on his intriguingly rugged profile. Taking advantage of his rapt concentration on the traffic, Mariah let her eyes have their fill. The kiss that she'd known they would inevitably share had been more explosively tumultuous than she'd ever imagined a kiss could be. Had he been as affected as she?

As though feeling her pondering gaze, David turned his sun-bronzed face toward her, a smile curving his sensuous lips. For a second their eyes met. And in that brief moment of contact, Mariah felt sure that he'd been as stirred by their embrace as she had been. As if to dispel any vestiges of uncertainty that might yet trouble her heart, his large hand captured hers as he turned his eyes back to the road. Without a word, he raised it to the heat of his lips.

Mariah's pulse quickened with excitement. She wanted to slide closer to him on the bench seat. She wanted to wrap her arms around his powerful biceps and lay her head on his shoulder, wanted to give in to the wonderful exhilaration of being with him.

But glancing once more at his tanned face silhouetted against the bright midday sun, Mariah's soaring elation was checked by wavering misgivings. Perhaps in her own heightened emotional state, she'd misread the message sent from those sea-green eyes of his.

Maybe he was only concerned that she had injured her foot and was being merely kind in taking her home. And face it, she told herself mercilessly, any moderately attractive woman who'd run to his work site and thrown herself into his arms as she had done could have expected to have been kissed with the same thoroughness. Maybe her own yearning desire had read more into his actions than he'd intended to convey. With an inward moan of self-recrimination Mariah pulled her hand from his.

She was too darned impetuous! When would she ever learn? If she'd practiced any self-control at all she wouldn't have humiliated herself twice in the same morning. Her mind seethed as she tried to focus her tear-filled eyes on the scenery passing swiftly outside her window. And she was sure the part about his wanting to hear about what had happened at the bank was true. Undoubtedly he'd be amused by how thoroughly she'd screwed up. He and Jeff Holden were close friends, weren't they? For all she knew her plan had been a joke to David too, a joke that he'd wanted to share with his buddy! Her glum thoughts kept her so occupied that she didn't even realize that they'd turned on to her street.

When they reached her apartment, David swung her up into his arms, ignoring her heated protests.

"Hey, what's the matter?" he asked, bewildered by her change in mood.

"I've made a fool of myself, that's what's the matter!" Mariah retorted hotly. "Me and my whole plan for a business are nothing but a joke to you, just like they were to Jeff Holden."

"Hold it. Hold it right there," David ordered, his face darkening grimly. "Nothing about you is a joke to me. It hasn't been from the moment I laid eyes on you. Now I don't know what that bonehead buddy of mine said to you, but I'm sure as hell going to find out. In the meantime you've got to believe that everything that's happened between us is real, at least on my part. Have you got that?"

Impaled by the full force of his green gaze, Mariah nodded weakly, believing him, totally accepting his words.

"Now that we have that straight," David's brow smoothed as his face relaxed into an intimate grin, "all you have to do is put those beautiful arms of yours around my neck and hold on. You're going for a ride."

Feeling suddenly secure, Mariah meekly complied, even going so far as to snuggle her face against the side of his neck as he effortlessly carried her up the three flights of stairs to her door. While still held in his strong arms, Mariah unlocked the door before

David solicitously carried her across the room and deposited her on the couch.

"Now let me take care of that puncture. Where is your first-aid kit?"

"I don't have a first-aid kit," Mariah said, laughing.

"Then how about some alcohol?"

"Scotch? Vodka? Gin?" she teased, pretending to misunderstand him.

"Denatured," he deadpanned.

"Really?" she joked. "I would have pegged you as a bourbon on the rocks man."

"You got that right," he went along with her, "but this time I'll stick to the cheaper stuff."

"That stuff is rotgut," she warned facetiously.

In silent reply his face assumed a mock glower.

"If you insist, look in the bathroom, in the medicine cabinet. But, David, I really don't need—" She broke off before finishing the sentence. He had already crossed the room and disappeared into the alcove.

Emerging almost immediately, bottle in hand, he unscrewed the cap and soaked a cotton ball.

"Hold out your foot," he directed before carefully and thoroughly daubing soaked cotton on her wound.

"Does it sting?" he asked.

"Don't feel a thing. I'm really not hurt at all."

"I can't take any chances," he declared seriously. "Superior Construction can't afford a lawsuit."

"A lawsuit!" Mariah howled. "Exhibit A!" She held up her foot. "A judge with twenty-twenty vision would need a magnifying glass to see where I'd been hurt if he were here right now!"

"People have sued for less," David remarked offhandedly before seating himself beside her. Then, lifting her legs and adjusting them across his hard, sinewy thighs, he went on gravely, "Have to elevate a wound."

Keeping his large hand cuddled around her calf he said, "Now that that's taken care of, tell me just what Jeff said to you about your loan."

"Are you sure you have time to listen right now?" Mariah asked anxiously, trying to squelch the disquieting emotions she felt at finding herself in such an intimate position with this undeniably attractive man. "Won't your boss dock your pay if you don't get back on the job?"

"Heck no," he assured her gravely. "I'm on the Superior payroll right this minute. This comes under Public Relations. It's a write-off."

"Public Relations? Oh, you mean about avoiding a lawsuit."

"Exactly."

"You think of me only as a member of the public?" Mariah asked coyly.

"Since I met you I've thought of you more as my private sector," David joked with a devilish chuckle.

She giggled at his play on words, as his hand slid boldly from her calf to her knee.

"You wanted to hear about my experience at the bank," she reminded him in a murmur, moistening her lips while attempting to restrain the quivering of her responsive body.

"Go ahead," he encouraged, a husky timbre in his voice, "tell me."

The heat of David's hand gradually making its way up her thigh was distracting. She couldn't concentrate.

"I'm trying to talk to you!" she protested feebly.

"I'm listening." His words were muffled against the skin of her bare shoulder as his lips brushed like a brand along her collarbone.

"David," she gasped. Her breathing seemed impaired. "I'm not getting the loan."

"Why not?" he asked musingly as his tongue drew circular patterns on the sensitive flesh of her upturned throat.

Thrusting her fingers into his thick shock of sun-bleached hair, Mariah closed them tightly and tugged his head up to where she could look into his eyes.

"Because I'm a quote, risk the bank is not willing to assume, unquote. My idea is quote, novel but untried, unquote, and I quote, lack business experience, unquote." She spoke rapidly, trying to get in all she had to say before his persistent strength managed to loosen her hold as he lowered his head to her breasts.

"So?" he inquired with infuriating calm as his hand beneath her skirt reached her hip then splayed maddeningly across her pulsing abdomen as his other arm encircled her shoulders pulling her tightly against him.

"So I'm still unemployed," she managed to say before his mouth crushed down on hers, hungrily parting her lips, his tongue driving urgently into its depths. With his lips clinging to hers, his hand found its way beneath the elastic of her waistband to caress the aching swell of her breasts.

She capitulated with a shuddering groan as his kiss deepened, driving from her mind any thoughts of Jeff Holden and the bank, quickening her desire until she was filled with only need—the need to touch

David as he was touching her, to run her hands along the muscles of his broad shoulders and sinewy back, to feel the taut planes of his flat abdomen, to press her thighs along the strong columns of his upper legs.

He pulled his lips from hers, his eyes dazed with desire. "Mariah, I need you," he whispered huskily.

"And I want you," she whispered back, suddenly surer than she'd ever been of anything in her life. Guiding his face back to hers, she boldly invaded his open mouth with her slender tongue.

She raised her body slightly to allow his hands to strip away her dress and lacy bikini. With a shattering groan his mouth left hers to move sensuously over her breasts as his fingers traced a teasing pattern up her inner thigh. Mariah was on fire with a consuming passion. She clawed at the knitted material stretched across his back—reached lower to tug relentlessly at the leather securing his faded jeans about his slim hips.

"Just a minute, honey," he drawled huskily.

Extricating himself from her clinging arms, he stood, towering above the couch. As he swiftly stripped the clothing from his magnificent body, Mariah stared in fascination at the perfection of his taut physique. In the full light of noon his tanned body appeared massive although not an ounce of fat marred his masculine beauty.

Arranging himself beside her on the deep-cushioned couch, he took her willing body into his arms, joining his mouth to hers in a deeply penetrating kiss. His hands explored the smoothness of her supple back, gently pressing her throbbing abdomen against his ready desire. A weakness flowed languidly down

76

her spine as her soft curves molded to fit his manly form.

The ripple of muscles beneath his smooth flesh excited her as she ran her hands down his tapering back to clutch his hard buttocks, urging him closer to her writhing hips.

"Mariah, honey, you're driving me over the brink." David's passion-thickened murmur was close to ear when at last he pulled his mouth from hers.

"Take me with you," she invited in a throaty voice she barely recognized as her own.

Holding her body with one powerful arm, he smoothly rolled them until Mariah found the couch cover beneath her back and David poised above her, his eyes shimmering like glittering emeralds in the sunlight.

She was on fire with yearning when at last he gently separated her thighs. Raising her buttocks slightly to receive his thrust, she cried out in pleasure as an explosion of sensation shook her slender frame when he entered her, filling her emptiness with vibrant strength. He covered her body with his, buried his face in the sensitive crook of her neck and shoulder, teasing her skin with his tongue.

Together in passion their rhythmic movements accelerated to a savage yet tender pitch. Locked in David's arms, sharing the ultimate expression of intimacy, Mariah experienced a oneness she'd never known. When together their feverish undulations reached the climactic union their ecstatic bodies sought, Mariah felt an overflowing happiness surge through her, canceling out all other earthly sensations.

She didn't know how long she remained suspended in the realm of pure elation. Time stood still. Then slowly she reeled back from the dizzy heights to become aware of David's powerful arms securely wrapped around her, his satisfying weight pressed closely along her body, the deep regular thud of his strong heart pounding against her breast.

Raising her weak hands to stroke his thick hair, her lips held an achingly sweet smile as she whispered, "That was good."

CHAPTER SIX

As soon as David heard the shower running, he picked up the phone and quickly dialed the bank.

"Holden, please, David Anthony calling," he requested quietly, his mouth close to the receiver.

It had been maddening to refuse Mariah's invitation to join her in the shower. He groaned inwardly remembering the sight of her raised eyebrow when he'd offered some feeble excuse about claustrophobia. What a jerk he must have appeared in her eyes! Actually he had no fear of confining places and there was no place he'd rather be than in the small steamy cubicle with her, his hands, slippery with soap lather, running smoothly over her delicious curves. A surge of desire shivered through him at the enticing thought, tempting him to slam down the receiver. But the memory of Mariah's abject disappointment and hot tears at being turned down for the loan to start her business kept him at the phone.

"Dave. What's up?" Jeff's voice boomed through the ear piece.

"I haven't got much time," David answered, his voice low, "so I'll get right to the point. When Mariah Benedict asked you for a loan this morning, I understand you turned her down. I'd like to know why."

"Good business, buddy, pure and simple. She's a fine-looking woman and I was sorry as hell to do it, but I had no choice. She didn't have any collateral, no business experience either. I'd be out on the street in no time if I lent money to every pretty face that asked me.

"I could tell she was upset. She came in with her head full of unrealistic expectations. It was too bad she didn't even stick around long enough for me to console her by asking her out to lunch," he said with a mock sigh. "Where did you meet her anyway? In a bar? Do you even really know her?"

"I know her," David assured him, a smile lighting his face as he remembered with pleasure just how well he knew her. "And forget any ideas of asking Mariah Benedict out to lunch," he added threateningly. "Is the Superior Construction account enough collateral for you?"

"What are you talking about?" Jeff asked. "You want to put a lien against your company to give her this loan?"

"If that's what it takes, that's exactly what I mean."

"Come off it, Dave. You and I both know you can write a check for the amount she's asking for out of your personal savings account. Or, if for some reason you don't want to do that, I can give you the money on a signature loan. With your net worth, you don't have to put up any collateral for a measly ten thousand dollars."

"Then take care of it. I wouldn't have sent her in to see you if I hadn't expected you to give her the loan. Just take the money out of my personal savings account, but don't let her know it's from me. Handle it through your accounts payable department. Let her think you reconsidered and had a change of mind."

"I don't know," Jeff drawled. "It's highly irregular. The auditor would have my neck."

"Don't be difficult. You know damn well it's not irregular," David said impatiently, hoping that Mariah was a woman who enjoyed the luxury of long showers. "You're the banker."

"Why don't you just give the money to her and leave me out of it?" Jeff asked.

"I'll explain later," David said, his voice full of irritation. "Just draw up the papers and I'll sign them. Call her today and tell her she can have the money."

"Not so fast. I've got to think about this. Hey, she isn't blackmailing you or anything, is she? Does that little blonde have something on you?"

"Of course not!" David exploded. "And don't think too long. If it takes you more than another thirty seconds to make up your mind, I'll be over to take all my accounts out of your bank and put them somewhere else."

"Hey, slow down!" Jeff protested. "Don't get so excited. You wouldn't do that! I'm the one who tipped you off to that old fellow who was on the verge of losing his broken-down duplex and just wanted someone to take it off his hands by paying the next month's rent. And I'm the one who refinanced that place after you got it fixed up so it was rentable, so you had the stake you needed to start your business. You've made a bundle, buddy, and I've stood behind you all the way, even when you were in some tight spots."

"Listen, *buddy*," David corrected swiftly, "it took a hell of a lot more than money to get me where I am.

81

Don't sit there and try to take all the credit for my success."

"I'm not," Jeff protested, "I'm just talking loyalty here. Besides, it's my job to give you financial advice from time to time. And I just can't understand this. You're so damned tight-fisted you've practically got the first dollar you ever earned. What I want to know is why you're suddenly so set on giving some of it away. It's out of character."

"I'm not giving it away," David growled. "I happen to think Mariah's worth the risk. In fact, it's not even a risk. She's come up with a unique idea and I know she's going to make a go of it. You're going to eat mud when she turns over her first profit, I'll see to that!"

"Okay, okay," Jeff put in placatingly. "I get the picture. I'll fix it up."

"Call her today. In fact, call her in about ten minutes, at home. You have her number handy?"

"Yeah, I stuck it in my wallet for further reference, if you know what I mean. But if I read you right, I guess I won't be needing it after this afternoon."

"You damn well won't!"

After hanging up the phone, David was relieved to hear that the shower was still running. It had been difficult enough to convince Jeff to go through with the unorthodox loan without having to come up with a plausible explanation to give Mariah if she'd caught him on the phone.

Blackmail! He snorted remembering Jeff's worried accusation. Still, he had to admit that Jeff had been right about it being out of character for him to easily part with any of his hard-earned money.

Feeling uneasy at Jeff's legitimate question about

why he didn't just give Mariah the money, David flinched inwardly. He was being devious, and it made him very uncomfortable. Mariah was so open and trusting he couldn't imagine her going behind anyone's back. And she had a streak of independence. She prided herself on being in control of her life and on being forthright. She wouldn't be happy at not knowing the truth. In fact, if she ever got wind of what he'd done, he knew she'd be damned mad, possibly so mad she'd never want to see him again.

It was a calculated risk. But he'd made his fortune on calculated risks and this was one he had to take. The simple truth was that he just wasn't ready yet to be completely honest with her. As far as she knew, he was an employee of the Superior Construction Company, not its owner, and, for the time being, he wanted to keep it that way.

But Mariah needed the money to get started and if she didn't start soon, she'd be back on the cocktail circuit. That was the last thing he wanted. There would be plenty of time later, after they knew each other better, to put his cards on the table.

He wanted to be sure of where he stood with her before she found out he was a wealthy man. He had been burned too many times before by women who thought they were going to get their hooks into him —and his money. In fact, he'd become so suspicious of friends who wanted to introduce him to their sisters or cousins that he'd practically stopped dating altogether. He'd deliberately kept a low profile.

He had no intention of getting tangled up with a calculated fortune hunter, but Mariah, with her sweet nature, could never be accused of being that. He knew he was hooked, a fish on the beautiful blonde's line, but the bait was so delicious that he was feeling no pain.

The spraying sound of the running water stopped abruptly, jolting him out of his thoughts and bringing him back to the reality of the beautiful woman behind the thin wall. A few quick strides took him back to the bed where he casually draped the rumpled sheet over his lower torso. When the door to the bathroom opened, he drew in his breath at the sight of Mariah toweling the moisture off her exquisite body. Her smile was all the invitation he needed to rise and wordlessly take the towel from her to gently finish the job.

Slowly his hands ran the towel over her breasts before cupping them together so that his searching tongue could moisten each rosy nipple again. As he gathered her to his chest, she felt the towel move sensuously down her back and over her hips. His mouth hungrily took her lips, causing her knees to weaken. Raising her damp arms, Mariah encircled his neck, her tongue seeking, searching into the depths of his mouth. A deep groan shuddered through him before the towel dropped to the floor. Then his arms enveloped her trembling body as his kiss became more demanding. She clung to him, lost in sensual delirium, aware of nothing but the magnificent man who could turn her blood to fire.

Holding her close with one arm, his other arm moved lower across her abdomen until his hand was between her thighs, possessively parting them, finding the tender flesh that was the essence of her passion. Writhing against his muscular body, Mariah felt herself coming to the point of reckless abandon. Her

84

fingers convulsively raked down his back, her nails leaving reddened trails on his bronzed skin.

From a long way off the ringing phone blended with the near-deafening beat of her heart.

"The telephone," David's husky voice whispered against her lips.

"Who cares?" her throaty voice answered.

"But it might be something important," he insisted, his breathing ragged against her cheek.

"Like a rug cleaner? Or a photographer?" Mariah asked, moving her hands to frame his face, trying to pull his mouth back on hers.

"Answer it," he commanded, swooping her up and carrying her across the room to the shrilling instrument.

Obediently, she lifted the receiver to her ear. "Hello," she nearly giggled as David's teeth tugged against one hardened nipple.

"Ms. Benedict? This is Jeff Holden, the loan officer you talked with earlier today."

"Yes, Mr. Holden," Mariah said loudly, suddenly sobering back to reality.

"I've been thinking about your proposition and there's something about it that I like. The uniqueness of the idea, I guess. Anyway, I've discussed the matter with, uh, another businessman who thinks you might have something there. And I've, uh, the bank, that is, has decided to back you in your little scheme."

For a moment Mariah was speechless. She didn't know how to react, what to say. She couldn't find the words she wanted. Jeff Holden's patronizing attitude was insulting. Her little scheme, indeed! If she didn't want this chance so badly, she would tell him what he

85

could do with his money! But the bank loan was the only way she would be able to get started, and Jeff Holden was offering her her chance. Most likely her only chance. But from what a source! Was it worth it?

Controlling her mounting ire, she forced her voice to answer sweetly, "Why, thank you, Mr. Holden. I appreciate your reconsideration."

"If you could get over here in an hour, Ms. Benedict, I'll have all the papers ready for you to sign. That way the transaction will clear the computer center before closing time and the money will be in your account by morning."

"I'll . . . I'll be there," Mariah assured him before reaching down to drop the receiver into its cradle.

"Holden?" David asked, snuggling his face into her neck. "He reconsidered?"

"Yes!" Mariah shrieked, throwing both her arms around David's shoulders. "I'm in business! The money will be in my account in the morning. Put me down. I have to get ready. I have to be at the bank in an hour."

"An hour? That'll give us time to finish our little unfinished business here." David smiled rakishly, tightening his hold.

"Not on your life! That can wait until later. I went into the bank this morning looking like a school kid. I'm going to need every minute to make myself presentable as a businesswoman," she argued firmly, squirming in his tight grasp, trying to free her body from his hold.

"Besides," she continued reasonably, "you've got to get ready too. You have to drive me. My car is back at your construction site, remember?"

"But . . ." David regretfully let her slide to her feet down his body and the evidence of his desire.

"Now, take a shower. A cold shower." Mariah giggled impishly, patting his distraught face.

Double-parked at the side of the bank building in the only shade available on the hot day, David kept the motor of his truck running. He couldn't see the entrance from where he waited, but when Mariah took a few steps out into the parking lot he knew he would be able to spot her.

He smiled, thinking of the way she had looked entering the bank. In her navy linen suit and high-necked ruffled blouse with her golden hair smoothed back into a bun, she looked every inch the successful executive. His face broke into a wide smile as he remembered her voiced regret that she didn't wear glasses since she felt they would give her a more intelligent look. As if she needed glasses! he thought. Her mobile face shone with continual evidence of her quick intellect.

Even the scarlet polish on her fingernails had been sacrificed to her new image. Although, he was happy to note, she had left her toenails brightly colored. Somehow, knowing that those toes glowed riotously inside her prim navy pumps made his heart beat a little faster.

She had wanted him to go in with her, but David had refused, unable to take a chance that either he or Jeff would tip their hand about the true identity of the backer of her loan. His relationship with Mariah had gotten off to a great beginning and he didn't want to throw any monkey wrenches into it by making her feel indebted to him.

She'd accepted him as a construction foreman and that was what he was going to remain until their relationship was on solid footing. If she found out that the apartment complex he was working on, as well as several others just as large scattered around the city, were his, he couldn't predict the obstacles that might prevent their really getting to know one another. There was a chance that nothing would change between them, but there was a chance that everything would. And, he thought as he squirmed uncomfortably, it was a chance he wasn't willing to take.

As the long, hot minutes dragged on, David became restless. After turning off the engine, he began to drum his fingers on the steering wheel. He still wouldn't put it past Jeff to make a play for Mariah. They had been rivals in love as far back as he could remember. There hadn't been a woman in the past that David had shown any real interest in that Jeff hadn't tried to win away from him.

Except for Carla, he remembered glumly. He should have known that when Jeff backed off there he wasn't being merely considerate. Unlike him, Jeff had been able to see Carla for what she was right from the start. And, like the good buddy he really was, Jeff had been the one who'd wised him up about Carla's shopping around for a new man to foot her bills when she'd figured that his money was running low.

It was just as well to play it cool for a while with Mariah. Though he was a decisive man who usually knew what he wanted when he saw it—and he was ninety-nine percent sure he wanted Mariah Benedict—there was always that chance that his instincts were wrong again. They'd sure as hell let him down when it came to Carla. No need to rush into any confessions, he thought once again, although the idea that he was being damned deceitful with the trusting, open Mariah made him uncomfortable.

"Hi." Mariah's voice jolted him from his reverie. She opened the door of the truck and climbed in, placing an impressive-looking packet on her lap.

"Did you sign your life away?" he asked lightly, turning the key in the ignition.

"No, I didn't! I've never been so surprised. Before when I've had to have a small loan, like when I bought my car or when I had to have a few hundred dollars to get it fixed, I've been given the third degree. Once I even had to get my boss to co-sign. This time I only had to sign a promissory note to get thousands of dollars."

"Then what took you so long?" David couldn't keep from asking.

"Well, I did have one embarrassing experience." Mariah blushed.

David saw red. Holden! He'd been a fool to think he could trust Holden alone with a woman who looked like Mariah. The damn skunk had made a pass at her. He'd wring his scrawny neck! In his rage it was a moment before he focused on her words.

"I had to fill out a personal-worth statement."

"Is that all?" David let out a relieved breath he had been unconsciously holding, privately damning himself for the jealous streak that led him to jump to conclusions.

"What did you expect?" Mariah asked innocently.

"I just can't see why you found that embarrassing."

"It sort of hurt to see that on paper I wasn't worth

very much. My car is so old it doesn't even have a blue book value!"

"What you're worth on paper doesn't mean a damn to me. And besides that will all soon change," he assured her, reaching over to take her hand. "What's all that stuff on your lap?"

"Isn't this great?" she asked proudly, taking her hand away to hold up a navy blue plastic zip case with the bank's name discreetly embossed in gold. "I really feel like a businesswoman now. Jeff gave me a complete set of amortization schedules. I didn't even know what that word meant until he explained that they were five-year, ten-year, and fifteen-year payback possibility schedules that I have to study to decide which one I'll need. And there's a rundown of state and federal tax regulations that I don't understand at all, but Jeff said he'd help me with them. And—"

"Jeff?" David asked, annoyed with himself at the peevish tone he heard in his own voice.

"Yes, Jeff," Mariah repeated, the smile leaving her face. "He calls me Mariah. Everyone at banks calls customers by their first names. Why shouldn't I call him Jeff?"

"I guess you're right." David sighed. "What else did Jeff do to help?" he asked, putting just a shade too much emphasis on the name.

"Jeff," Mariah retorted mockingly, "gave me a list of car dealerships that lease vehicles and gave me a rundown on which cars he thinks are the most reliable according to consumer research. You know, it's strange, but he almost seemed like a different person this afternoon. I can understand now how the two of you could be friends. Given the chance I think I could like the guy. Oh, and he also had a few helpful suggestions for services I could offer."

"I'll just bet he did," David said sarcastically.

"David," Mariah rebuked, surprise widening her eyes, "I think you're jealous."

"I am not," he protested, although the word rankled unpleasantly. "It's just that a few hours ago he was Mr. Holden and you were calling him a snake. Now it's 'Jeff' this and 'Jeff' that. Why the big change of attitude?"

"Because, somehow, I feel he's responsible for giving me my chance."

"Correction, it's the bank, not Mr. Holden, that's lending you the money."

"I'm not so sure about that," Mariah remarked reflectively. "That bank loan was more like a personal loan than a business loan."

"Have you ever had a business loan before?" David challenged.

"No," Mariah answered after a thoughtful silence.

Damn that Holden, David thought irritably. First interrupting a very pleasant afternoon by insisting that she come right down to the bank, then somehow giving Mariah the idea that *he* was her benefactor, and now causing what sounded dangerously close to an argument between them.

"Well," David stated truthfully, "a business loan is much easier to get than a personal loan." If you have enough collateral, he added silently. "And as for Jeff being your co-signer, I doubt that very seriously. That guy has all his money invested in high-yield bonds. In fact, a hell of a lot of it is my money, since I've always ended up paying for dinner or drinks because he had either left his checkbook home, not had any change, or made up some other stupid excuse." Damn! David sounded petty even to his own ears, but he was helpless to stop himself.

"Whatever." Mariah shrugged, summarily dismissing his statement. "I can't understand why you're putting him down so, since the two of you are supposedly such good friends. And no matter what you say, I still think Jeff is more involved in this than you'd like me to believe."

"And how does that make you feel?" David demanded.

"At first I didn't much like the idea. I was even tempted to ask him if he was. But then I remembered how angry I was at him this morning and how helpless I felt when he turned me down, and I didn't want to risk losing the deal. I really believe that I'm going to make a success out of this. And Jeff does too. Wherever the money is coming from, I'm grateful for it. It's the only way I can get started. I intend to pay back every cent of it—with interest. And as quickly as I can, I'm going to amortize my debt," she added, savoring the new word.

She was some woman, David thought. He admired her spunk and practical reasoning. "And I believe you're going to make a go of it too," he remarked convincingly.

"Oh David, I never would have even gotten my idea off the ground if it hadn't been for you. I'd still be sitting around in my apartment trying out new hairstyles and giving myself oatmeal facials until it was time to collect next week's unemployment check!

"You're the one with all the really good suggestions for how to get started. How could I have gone in that bank and talked about PCs and advertising expenses, and all that if it hadn't been for you?" Her eyes shining with emotion, she moved close beside him, hugging his arm tightly against her firm breast.

"You're the person I need more than any other," she declared vehemently. Her impulsive gesture raised his temperature to near the boiling point, though her statement effectively smothered the embers of his smoldering jealousy.

"Would you like to go somewhere for a cool drink to celebrate?" he asked, dropping a light kiss on her fragrant hair.

"No, thanks. I'm afraid I don't think of going to a bar or a lounge as a treat," she said gently.

"Oops, sorry about that." David grinned ruefully. "I imagine you don't. Well then, what do you have in mind?"

"Just stop at the little market by my place," she answered with a smile. "I need to pick up a few things for dinner. Then I just want to get home and take these clothes off."

"Great idea!" his voice brightened. "I've been thinking about the same thing myself."

"What? About going to the grocery store?" Mariah teased.

"Whatever." He shrugged. "If that's where you want me to take your clothes off, I'm game."

CHAPTER SEVEN

"Hey, you procrastinator, got any room in your busy life for me?" Mariah lip-synched to her own voice coming from the stereo speakers of her sleek silver-gray Supra as she sped along the freeway. "Think how great you'd feel to have that package you've been meaning to mail to your mom at the post office right now! And what about that suit jacket or dress hanging in your closet with the price tags still attached? You know, the one that isn't the color you thought it was when you bought it, or that doesn't fit just right across the shoulders. Wouldn't you be relieved to have it returned to the store and off your charge?

"Do you really enjoy standing in those lines to pay your traffic fines? Or to buy the license tags you've put off getting so long that now it's too late to mail in for them?

"Of course you don't! But I do! I'll pick up your dry cleaning, return those rented videos gathering dust on your bookshelves, or stand in line for great tickets to that very popular concert you've been waiting to go to for months. I'll even pay your taxes, get building permits, and grocery shop for that impromptu dinner you impulsively but unwisely invited the

94

gang to last night! How about gassing up your car and getting the tires checked for that weekend trip you've planned? Whatever it is that your time is too valuable to waste on standing in line, I'll be glad to take over for you.

"Let me do the running around so you can meet your important deadlines without all that worry. Isn't it worth a little something to have that guilt trip lifted from your already overloaded mind? A reasonable set fee and mileage is all it will cost for you to really be able to enjoy this beautiful day. Just call Mariah at 926-H-E-L-P. Help! Remember, I'm here to make things easier for you."

"Say, Mariah, do you clean closets? Recycle cans? Bake sugar cookies like Mom used to?" the disc jockey quipped before he started another popular recording.

Mariah had to smile as she slowed for the off ramp. It had taken two days of rewrites, revisions, and careful rehearsing to get everything she'd wanted to say boiled down to where it made sense and fit into the ninety-second commercial. She'd wanted to end her advertisement saying, "I'm here for you!" But David had objected so seriously and strongly to that statement that in the end she had compromised.

She could hardly believe that after only two months her business had caught on so well that she only had to run the commercial once a week. One advertising spot on the popular station that was listened to by well-heeled commuters brought in more than enough business to keep her running nearly twelve hours a day for the following week. Then, of course, there were the repeat customers, a special clientele she was beginning to build up who had her scheduled to run errands for them on a regular basis. Ones like the owner of the two poodles obediently sitting on the backseat of her car, patiently awaiting their bimonthly grooming appointment at Pete's Poodle Parlor which was now just around the corner.

She would drop off the twin curly-haired miniatures and swing around to 21st Street to pick up Mrs. Snyder's glasses from the optometrist. Then she would go on to get prescriptions filled at the hospital pharmacy for several shut-ins and pick up the medical research books from the hospital's library that were on hold for a university student, before getting the signed papers an escrow company needed immediately from a procrastinating second mortgage holder who was delaying an important deal. Then she would return to pick up the dogs and take them home before starting out for her errands on the other side of town.

Mariah loved her new job. She loved the kind of people she met now. And she loved the freedom of wheeling her new car down the obscure streets into little-known neighborhoods, getting to know the city as she had never known it before.

It was also exciting to be out among the busy crowds in the stores or on the streets in the daylight hours. She hadn't been able to do that for the past several years. Her job as a cocktail waitress had kept her up late with the nighttime people. She was a morning person, no doubt about that, she thought as she remembered the thrill she experienced of waking early knowing that she had a full and prosperous day before her. While she'd been living through those years she hadn't realized just how oppressive it

America's most popular, most compelling romance novels...

Here, at last...love stories that really involve you! Fresh, finely crafted novels with story lines so believable you'll feel you're actually living them! Characters you can relate to...exciting places to visit...unexpected plot twists...all in all, exciting romances that satisfy your mind and delight your heart.

had been to live her life on a daily schedule that went against her body's natural bio-rhythms.

And, even more important, now when she awoke in the early morning she had the luxury of being swept into David's waiting arms. She smiled dreamily, remembering the wonderful way she'd started her day. Incredibly, David was a morning person too. At night when he came home after the sun had set, he had little energy left other than what it took to get himself into the shower before eating a late dinner. He was too tired from the rigors of his fourteen-hour day to do more than hold her close while they looked at a little TV snuggled up on her couch-turned-bed.

But early morning was a different story altogether! Stopped by a red light, Mariah glanced shyly at the occupant of the car next to her, whose eyes were firmly fastened on the light, almost fearing that her thoughts could be read on her face. What energy David had then! And tenderness too. She knew that in her life to come, no matter what happened between them, whenever the dawn started breaking, prompting the myriad of summer birds in the leafy trees to begin their morning serenade, she would be reminded of the consuming sweetness of her affair with David Anthony.

One evening toward the end of August, as David sat on the small balcony of Mariah's apartment resting in the cool, star-studded evening, he realized suddenly that things had changed. More often than not the past two weeks, or possibly even three, he wrinkled his brow trying to remember, the evening meal that Mariah had waiting for him had come from the local deli. They must have gone through the place's lim-

97

ited menu at least twice, he thought, since this was the third time they'd had the same lasagna and pickled mushrooms.

And they hadn't had an uninterrupted meal for as long as he could remember. During each meal the unpleasant sound of Mariah's beeper sounded at least twice, summoning her to the phone to call her answering service. Tonight had been particularly annoying. There had been four calls. He'd been left to eat his dinner alone while Mariah made arrangements and punched her appointments into her computer.

The last interruption that had him out on the balcony alone had really ticked him off. He'd been right in the middle of trying to get her to make a commitment to go away for the long Labor Day weekend, but he hadn't gotten to first base when that damn beeper had started, interrupting their conversation. True, he was being rather devious, not coming straight out with his plans because he wanted to surprise her, but it was still frustrating to have his every mention of a mini-vacation thwarted by her quick claims that she couldn't leave her booming but still fledgling business for four or five days.

"Oh, David," Mariah's lilting voice rang out as she dropped into the chair beside him. "I'm so excited. That was the sweetest woman on the phone. She wants me to stand in line tomorrow to buy a whole block of concert tickets to the laser rock show that will be here for only one night next week. From all the publicity, it's going to be the hottest thing to hit town all summer. I'm going to have to get up really early for that one. I've already had several calls from regular clients to get tickets for them, too."

98

"So?"

"What do you mean 'so?'" Mariah mimicked his petulant question. "For one thing, I would have had to turn down the job a week ago because I wouldn't have had enough in my account to buy that many tickets, and my business is going so well that now I do. You know it's been hard sometimes for me to spend my money and take the chance that I might not be reimbursed, but I really have no choice. I certainly can't run around collecting the cash before performing the service. That would double my expenses and cut the amount I could accomplish with my time in half."

"So?" he repeated, almost as though he intended to irritate her.

"And, so, for the second thing, it's a senior citizen group that's going!"

David was silent.

"What's wrong with you tonight? Don't you think it's great they're interested in going?"

"Of course I do," David remarked, trying but not managing to sound enthusiastic. "But I'd rather discuss our plans for next week than a bunch of senior citizens who want to risk losing what little hearing they might have left at a rock concert."

"That's unkind, David, and very unlike you to say something like that. I know you don't mean it. What's bothering you anyway?" She reached out and gently took his callused hand in hers.

He let out a deep sigh. "Ever since we met we haven't had a chance to take any time off except Sundays—"

"And we usually spend them in bed," Mariah interrupted with an engaging laugh, giving his hand an intimate squeeze.

"True," he admitted, smiling in the darkness. "But now that I've managed to get several days ahead of schedule because of the dry weather we've had this month, we have a chance to really go someplace. My —uh, friend, has a yacht, and I thought we could take a cruise up around the San Juan Islands for a few days."

"Your friend? Jeff?"

"No, not Jeff." David could hear the curtness in his answer. Then contritely softening his tone, he explained, "It's a guy whom I've built several apartment complexes for."

"It would be nice to meet some of your friends," Mariah mused. "We've both been so busy this summer we haven't had time for much else than each other, have we?"

"We wouldn't be going with my friend," David hastily amended. "There'd only be the two of us."

Raising her hand to his lips, he kissed her smooth skin. Why didn't he just come out and tell her it was his boat and that it needed a good run to keep it in shape? he wondered. Why was he keeping up this pretense of being a day laborer? Why couldn't he tell her that when this job was done, he was going to retire from actual physical participation in the construction business and that he was ready to begin a new life—a new life, he was almost sure, that would center around her?

"It sounds wonderful." He heard her sigh. "I've always wanted to go on a boat trip. When I worked at a lounge down on the waterfront, people used to tie up their yachts at the pier and come into the restau-

100

rant for dinner. Imagine, they'd drive up in their big boats just for the evening." She gave another sigh that was soft as the evening breeze.

"We'll 'drive up' to every restaurant between here and Friday Harbor," he promised softly.

"Is it a big boat?" Mariah asked wistfully.

"A very big boat," David assured her with a grin, beginning to hope that the tide was turning his way. But his hopes were dashed with her next words.

"I'd love to," Mariah said, "but I can't. I've got a long list of cars I'm gassing up on that Friday. That's all I'll be doing that day. Then Saturday I know I'll be busy exchanging kids' clothes for all the mothers who couldn't stand the idea of taking their kids shopping and who've just discovered the things they bought aren't the right size for the little darlings to wear on the opening day of school. Besides that, I'll be making my regular video drops and pickups." She removed her hand from his and patted his knee. "By the way, thanks for suggesting the video rental idea. That's turned into a real lucrative service."

"Too lucrative," he muttered.

"Don't be like this!" Mariah exclaimed in frustrated tones. "I want you to be proud of me. After all, that was one of your own ideas."

"I am proud of you and the way you're building up your clientele. But you can't work all the time."

"Look who's talking!"

"I work hard in the summer, but only because I know I'll have time for myself in the winter. This thing that you've got going looks like it's going to take over your life."

"And I love it!"

More than you love me? The question ran unbidden through his mind. And though the words were on the tip of his tongue, he couldn't say them. Not yet. He didn't want anything to threaten their developing relationship. Not the admission that the yacht was his. Not the admission that he was the one backing her promising enterprise. Certainly not the admission that he was totally in love with her.

"Let's just drop the subject, shall we?" His words were spoken more gruffly than he intended and he gave an inward groan when she abruptly removed her hand from his knee.

The instant David's eyes opened the next morning to the dawn's first gray light he realized he was alone. Quickly sitting up, he saw a note lying on Mariah's pillow. Picking it up, he lay back down to read:

Had to go. I couldn't sleep for worrying all night that I might not be able to get a whole section of tickets if I wasn't the first in line. See you tonight and I promise a real home cooked meal.

The note was covered with rosy imprints of Mariah's lipsticked mouth. And when he got up he saw in the bathroom mirror that she'd pressed another pink kiss on his forehead. The imaged imprint wrinkled as his brow furrowed. It was one thing for Mariah to make a modest success of her brainchild business, he thought, but quite another when it grew to such proportions that it began to seriously interfere with his personal life. Then he groaned as the irony hit him: before Mariah, he hadn't really had a personal life.

As David showered and dressed without even a cup of hot coffee to get himself moving, he knew he was behaving childishly. There was no reason he couldn't start the coffee maker. He'd done it countless times in the lonely years before he'd known Mariah. And there was no reason for him to resent Mariah's success. He had to shape up and quit feeling sorry for himself, he thought sternly. Wasn't Mariah exactly the woman he'd envisioned as the one to share his assured and prosperous life? And more, he answered his own question. He'd never dreamed that all that ambition and drive could come in such a gorgeous package with a loving nature and sense of humor thrown in to boot.

He was a damned lucky guy to have her, he concluded as he slammed the door shut behind him.

The driving rain beat down on Mariah, plastering her hair to her scalp as she stood outside the coliseum on the Saturday night of the laser rock concert desperately trying to sell the block of tickets she had purchased for the senior citizen group.

The earlier scene with David ran through her painfully throbbing head.

"What do you mean they aren't going to buy the tickets?" he'd demanded.

"When I delivered them to the address that lovely woman had given me, I found out it was a nursing home!" she'd wailed.

"So?" he'd asked in that syllable that was beginning to get on her nerves.

"So—when I talked to the director of the home, he doubled over in laughter. It seems that Mrs. Wilson, as sweet as she is, is rather senile. Though she may have thought it was a good idea for her whole wing from the nursing home to go to the concert on the night when she watched the ad on TV—if you'll remember it played right before that little advertising spot I tried that week—when we questioned her she had no recollection that she'd ever called me! The director wasn't very sympathetic. The thought of all those senior citizens wheeling into a rock concert seemed more than he could handle."

"But what are you going to do with the tickets?"

"I guess I'll advertise them in the personals and what I don't sell that way, I'll have to sell at the gate."

"But isn't that illegal?"

"Illegal? How can it be?"

"Isn't ticket scalping something you can get arrested for?"

"I'm not a scalper!" she'd protested. "I'll sell them for exactly what I paid for them."

"Sell them to me," David had offered. "I'll hand them out to the guys at work. And any videotapes that are overdue on Saturday, I'll pay for too. All I care about is you and me getting away together without that damn telephone interrupting every five minutes. We need time to ourselves. Doesn't our relationship mean anything to you?"

"Of course it does, David. How can you even ask that? But this is business and I've got to take care of it myself. I got into this mess all on my own and I don't expect anyone to bail me out. Especially not you, the way you work for your hard-earned money. It's completely out of the question! You go on your boat trip. I'll stay here and handle this."

So there she was on Saturday night, with a pounding headache, hawking tickets in the first torrential rain the city had had all summer long. The chill wind with its suggestion of autumn threatened to turn her umbrella inside out. Her mood was as dismal as the weather. In spite of all her efforts, she'd only managed to get rid of five tickets so far. Maybe, she decided, if she moved up under the overhang and held out the tickets so that people could see what she was trying to sell she'd do better.

She laboriously squirmed her way through the boisterous crowd toward the protection the circular marquee offered. She grew hoarse, arguing and explaining her predicament every inch of the way to the irate concertgoers who thought she was trying to jump the line and who weren't above jabbing her with an elbow or sticking out a shoulder to block her passage.

Finally, feeling bruised and battered from head to toe, after she'd found a spot where she could safely take out the tickets to display them, she called out, "I have twenty tickets for the concert that I'd like to sell."

Mariah saw almost immediately that this tack wasn't going to get her anywhere. In the din, only the nearest people could hear her. An eerie picture of the nursing home inhabitants wrapped in lap robes, sitting in their wheelchairs among this crowd superimposed itself on her brain, causing her to shake her head slightly. David had been right from the first. Why hadn't she listened to his reservations about the whole idea? Why hadn't she checked out Mrs. Wilson's request and gotten the money before she bought the tickets?

Hindsight was clear, but Mariah reminded herself she had to deal with the present. Maybe, if she could somehow manage to balance herself on one of the

105

curving pylons supporting the building, she could make herself heard by more people.

Precariously finding a toehold on the large rivets protruding from the steel I-beam, Mariah managed to climb a foot or more off the ground. Clinging to the wet metal with one arm, she waved the other with a handful of tickets above her head. "Tickets," she yelled. "Who would like to buy a ticket?"

Then the sole of her jogging shoe slipped and she dropped to the ground with a bone-jolting thud. Only a strong hand that fastened firmly around her arm kept her from falling on her face. Gratefully turning to thank her rescuer, she gaped in astonishment. The uniformed man with the silver badge pinned to his blue shirt was a policeman.

"Come along, lady, you're under arrest."

"What for?" Mariah managed to stammer as he resolutely pulled her through the opening the curious crowd made for them.

"Ticket scalping. I'll read you your rights in the patrol car."

"But I'm not a scalper," she protested, trying to quell her rising panic. Why hadn't she listened to David? Why had she dismissed his comments so lightly? She should have asked him all he knew about the laws concerning scalpers. "I'm selling the tickets for what I paid for them."

"They all say that," the officer said dispassionately. "Tell it to the judge."

He didn't loosen his grip on her upper arm until he placed her in the backseat of the black and white car with its ominous blue light flashing on the roof. Mariah pulled the lapels of her soggy ski jacket up around her face, trying to shield herself from the curious glances of onlookers, hoping no one she knew would see her as the officer read her her rights before he closed her door.

As he went around the car to the front passenger side, Mariah searched frantically for the door handles, hoping she could jump out of the vehicle and get away. But there were no handles on either door and banging with both fists on the thick glass between her and the two men up front proved hopeless. It was soundproof and undoubtedly bulletproof, too. Never had she felt more helpless or wronged.

CHAPTER EIGHT

"David?" Mariah wailed into the telephone in the busy police station. "They're going to put me in jail!"

"Where are you? What happened? Have you been arrested?" His succinct questions came in rapid-fire succession.

"They think I'm a scalper! I'm not and you know it. Yes, they arrested me. They even read me my rights, just like on television. Please come down here and tell them I'm an honest woman! Please," she pleaded.

Turning toward the counter, she tried vainly for a little privacy, thanking her lucky stars that he'd decided not to go on the boat trip without her. Just what would she have done then? Funny, before she'd met David she'd been perfectly capable of handling all her problems herself. Of course, ever since she'd met him her problems had become more complicated!

"Hang in there, honey. I'll be there as fast as I can. Where are you?"

"I don't know." Mariah fought back the sob that threatened to escape her throat. "I was so ashamed I kept my head down the whole drive here. I didn't pay any attention to where they were taking me.

This is like a bad dream, but I pinched myself and I didn't wake up."

"Find out where you are," David repeated.

"Just a minute and I'll see if someone will tell me."

Turning aside to address the uniformed matron standing inches from her, Mariah asked, "Where am I?"

"The city jail," the muscular woman answered grimly.

"The city jail," Mariah repeated into the phone, hysteria mounting in her breast. "Please hurry. I've already been fingerprinted and they took mug shots of me. Now they're going to lock me up." Her voice rose uncontrollably.

"I'll be right there, honey. I'll take care of you. Don't worry."

"Just hurry, David, I don't know how much more I can stand."

Hearing the phone go dead at the other end, Mariah slumped against the counter, realizing with awful certainty that nothing stood between her and the confinement she dreaded.

"Come on, Benedict," the matron said as she took the phone from Mariah's limp hand and placed it in the cradle. "I haven't got all night." She pointed toward a narrow corridor and motioned Mariah to start walking.

"Wait, please, you can't lock me up. I haven't done anything wrong." Mariah tried to control her shaking voice.

"Forget it, Benedict," the woman remarked unsympathetically. "That's what they all say."

Mariah held out one arm in an effort to halt the woman's impatient expression. Swallowing with effort, she cleared her throat and pitched her voice an octave lower.

"I was only selling the tickets at cost. I wasn't trying to make money. Only to get back my investment. You see, I have a business where I . . ." Mariah stopped in mid-sentence, becoming aware that nothing she could say would make an impression on the impassive face before her.

"Let's go, Benedict," the woman ordered.

Sighing with resignation, Mariah turned and dejectedly moved in the direction the woman had indicated, the sound of the matron's footsteps heavy behind her.

Turning her head to talk over her shoulder, Mariah pleaded, "You don't have to put me in a cell. I'll be good. Just let me sit out there on the bench in the room where the man took my statement."

But her words fell on deaf ears. The woman didn't even bother to answer nor slow her plodding step.

When they arrived at a cell containing three women, the matron unlocked the door and slid it slightly ajar before reaching out to take Mariah's arm. Mariah flinched away from the woman's touch and tentatively stepped over the threshold into the cell. The barred door swung shut behind her with a clang.

"Please, Sir, I mean Miss—Officer? Let me know when my friend, David Anthony, gets here. I have to talk to him right away."

"You'll have your chance to see him before your arraignment in night court. If he shows," the woman added without looking at her.

Then it was silent except for the dull sound of the

matron's unhurried footfalls receding down the long corridor.

"Of course, he'll come," Mariah shouted indignantly after her, when the woman's words had had time to sink into her dazed brain. Grasping the bars, she tried to shake the immovable door in her frustration. She had to hold on to that knowledge! Only the certainty that David would be there warmed her frightened heart.

As Mariah stood holding the cold steel bars of her cage she felt heavy hands on her shoulders. Whiskey-laden breath wheezed close to her ear.

"Come on, honey," the voice rasped, "it's gonna be okay. Take the load off your feet. Oops . . ."

Mariah turned, shrugging away from the offensive embrace, and saw an older woman weave uncertainly toward a builtin metal cot on the far wall of the cell. Oblivious to the fact that the cot was already occupied, the slovenly woman lurched toward the narrow space between two younger women who sat there. They rose, disgust clear on their faces, and languidly walked toward Mariah.

Their overdone makeup was noticeable even in the dim light of the cell, and although it was still summer both of them wore white leather boots on their shapely legs below very short, tight black leather skirts. Their blouses were sleeveless, low cut and almost transparent. When they came up to her, Mariah could see goose bumps prickling the skin of both women's arms. Mariah could sympathize with their discomfort because the air conditioning blowing full blast into the cell was unpleasantly ruffling her own still damp hair and clothing.

"Well, what do we have here?" the blonde remarked to the brunette as the women stood, their eyes glittering in their sullen faces, taking in Mariah from head to toe.

Mariah took their impudent scrutiny for a minute or two, staring back at them with as much curiosity as they seemed to be deriving from their study of her. Her first impression had been that the women were older than she, but up close she could tell they were young, very young. She would guess somewhere around twenty. Their skin under their heavy makeup was unlined and nearly flawless. The impression of age, she realized, came from the world-weary look in their hardened gazes. She shivered slightly. Between them the two appeared as though they'd seen every seedy thing there was to see. Strangely, although their pointed interest was far from friendly, Mariah did not feel menaced.

"How long do you think we'll be in here?" Mariah ventured, her voice faltering.

"Depends," the brunette answered, her voice surprisingly high. "Got a cigarette on you? Or did they strip search you?"

"Strip search?" Mariah shrieked, a shudder convulsing her frame at the repulsive thought. Could that be yet to come? Surely not for a simple charge of ticket scalping. But just how simple was it? she wondered. For the first time the possibility of fines and even a real prison sentence occurred to her. How on earth had she ever ended up in a jail cell when she could have so easily been out on the Sound, resting in the security of David's strong arms, rocked to sleep by the gentle motion of the water?

"Come off it," the bleached blonde retorted, her

voice heavy with sarcasm. "The cigarettes . . . you got some?"

"I don't smoke," Mariah said, feeling hopelessly out of her element as a new panic rose within her.

The blonde let out a derisive snort and sauntered back to the single cot on which the drunken woman had crumpled. Mariah watched as she gave the woman a jab, making her move enough so that the girl could sit down. But the brunette stayed at Mariah's side.

"Why don't they have enough beds in here for each of us?" Mariah asked. "Or at least chairs so we could sit down?" She shuddered once more, catching sight of the open toilet in the corner of the room. It was unbelievable. Anyone who happened by could catch sight of them using the john!

"This is just a holding tank. They're not too worried about our comfort. Although I can't say the regular cells are any different except they have a cot for each person. You never been in here before?" the girl asked.

"No." Mariah shook her head dejectedly.

"What d'you get picked up for?" the brunette asked, unable to conceal her curiosity.

Mariah considered her answer. She desperately wanted to know what was going to happen to her in this fearful place and this was one person who might be able to tell her. She had never realized how limited her knowledge of jails actually was. Should she admit to the charge of ticket scalping in order to establish some sort of rapport with her cell mate, who obviously knew the ropes? No, somehow she couldn't do it. She was innocent of any wrongdoing and this whole nightmare was a demeaning mistake.

113

"I didn't do anything wrong. I'm innocent and my friend will be here any minute to get me out of here." The sound of her own words and the thought of David rushing to her rescue bolstered Mariah's wilted confidence.

"Yeah, sure," the brunette said, hostilely dismissing her to go join her friend at the back of the cell.

Mariah stayed at the bars, gripping them so tightly that her fingers grew numb. As her ears strained for a sound in the silent corridor, her rampant mind imagined all sorts of horrible scenarios. She vividly pictured David in a car crash caused by his haste to rescue her. She saw herself condemned to months in jail while he lay comatose in his hospital bed.

Tears rose in her eyes and a sob tore from her throat.

A key jangled in the lock, bringing Mariah back to reality. Hastily she wiped her eyes on her sleeve as the door slid open.

"Mariah Benedict," the matron intoned. "Follow me."

"Where are you taking me?" Mariah asked fearfully as she walked behind the stolid, uniformed back, wondering if the dreaded strip search or some other awful humiliation was next.

But the woman didn't answer. Long moments passed before Mariah found herself escorted into a room with rows of wooden benches arranged like church pews in front of a raised and fenced-off podium. A robed judge seated behind it was leaning forward, engaged in deep conversation with two rather rowdy-looking men.

The matron ordered Mariah to sit on the front bench, then went to stand at the back of the room.

Oh, David, where are you? Mariah cried inwardly, turning to look around the stark, windowless room, beginning to fear that perhaps something terrible had actually happened to him.

As if in answer to her fervent question, the door swung open and David walked in, swiftly covering the distance between them with long strides. Sliding onto the bench beside her, he gathered her into his arms.

"I'm so glad you're all right," she whispered against his shoulder. "I'd never have forgiven myself if anything had happened to you."

"Me?" he questioned. "What are you talking about, honey? You're the one on trial. Now, don't worry. I took the time to phone my lawyer. After calling the station to get the details of the arrest he said that you probably wouldn't need him. The evidence is circumstantial, since you weren't caught in the act of selling. His advice was to tell the truth in a straightforward manner."

Relaxing against David's strength, assured by his calm disclosure, Mariah knew that later there would be time to explain her hysterical apprehensions for his safety. She rested her head against his neck as he continued speaking.

"He also said you're lucky to go up before the judge who's on the bench tonight. It seems he's the most compassionate night court judge, especially in cases where the defendant doesn't have a prior record." David paused almost imperceptibly. "You don't, do you?"

Mariah jerked free of his embrace, confronting his gaze with hers. "Don't what?"

"Have a record," David repeated resolutely, his face immobile and devoid of emotion.

"David Anthony, how could you ask such a thing?"

"I don't know," he said awkwardly. "It just suddenly occurred to me that you might have an outstanding traffic ticket . . . something like that."

"Well, I don't!" Mariah assured him with a vehemence that left no room for doubt. Deciding to forgive him for posing the question, she let her shoulder relax against his. "I've never even gotten a parking ticket! And, believe me, this is my last brush with the law. It's been awful!"

"Poor baby," David murmured, putting his arm back around her. "It'll soon be over. It looks as though Judge Wilson might be ready to get the show on the road."

Judge Wilson? Mariah's active mind caught fearfully at the name. Mrs. Wilson was the little old woman who had inadvertently gotten her into this mess. There was no way she could feel as confident as David did that a judge by the same name would get her out of it. Instead, Mariah's spirits fell. It was as if she'd been double jinxed.

"Mariah Benedict," the judge called out, as the two men standing before him shook hands and walked down the aisle appearing a little chagrined, but wearing relieved smiles on their swollen and bruised faces.

Mariah stood and uncertainly advanced toward the railing where she was sworn in by the bailiff.

"Ms. Benedict," Judge Wilson said, looking at her not unkindly. "You've been charged with the illegal sale of tickets outside the coliseum in a restricted zone. Do you plead guilty or not guilty?"

Helplessly Mariah looked behind her toward David. Was she guilty? She had sold two tickets, but not at the place the police had apprehended her. David's encouraging smile braced her trembling knees.

Turning back to the judge, she made her decision. "Not guilty," she asserted firmly.

"The police officers who brought you in claim that you had climbed onto the girders of the coliseum to hawk your wares," the gray-haired judge remarked, his gaze scanning a document before him. Looking up, he asked, "Don't you think that was a rather blatant flaunting of the law?"

"I don't think I'm guilty of doing anything illegal," Mariah answered, adding uncertainly, "Your Honor."

"Then why don't you tell me your version of the story, young lady?" the judge invited, settling back into his large leather seat, running his thumb and forefinger up and down the smooth surface of a gold pen he held.

Mariah took a deep breath before plunging in. The judge just had to understand!

"Thank you, Your Honor. You see I was just trying to get some of my own money back since a customer who'd asked me to buy the block of twenty-five tickets for her was unable to pay for them. You can call the Mountain and Sound View Nursing Home . . . they'll tell you the whole story. It was a woman there, a resident, who ordered the tickets."

"Mountain and Sound View?" the judge inquired with interest, as though he recognized the name. "Why would anyone at the nursing home want twenty-five tickets for a rock concert? I don't believe there's anyone in the place under seventy-five years of age."

"I didn't know the address was a nursing home when I bought the tickets. I only found that out when I delivered them. I guess I was naïve, but I thought it was wonderful that senior citizens wanted to get out and keep abreast of the latest trends. Funny coincidence, but it was a Mrs. Wilson who ordered them." She glanced up at the judge, who sat bolt upright in his seat. "She was a charming woman. I really liked her when she called, and it never occurred to me that she wouldn't pay for the tickets.

"But when I got to the home and talked to Mrs. Wilson I realized that she didn't even remember calling me. After the director pointed out that she wasn't always responsible for her actions, I didn't feel right about making her pay for them. I told the director I'd sell them to someone else.

"I thought I could sell them by advertising in the paper, but that didn't pan out. You see, my business, Procrastinators Unlimited, is new and I couldn't afford the loss. When my ad didn't work I had to go to the concert to see if I could sell some of them there. I didn't think it was scalping because I wasn't selling them for one cent over what I had paid for them."

"A Mrs. Wilson, you say, at the Mountain and Sound View Home?" A smile tugged at the corners of the judge's lips. "Ms. Benedict, I'd appreciate it if you and your friend," he gestured toward David, "would join me in my chambers. I think that if we put our minds to it we can clear this matter up."

As soon as the door shut behind Mariah and David, the judge motioned them to comfortable seats.

"I'm indeed sorry for your inconvenience, but I'm

118

afraid there's no way I can truly make it up to you," Judge Wilson remarked.

David shrugged his shoulders in answer to Mariah's questioning glance when the judge turned his back to them. Opening a closet he took a checkbook from the jacket pocket of a suit coat hanging there before seating himself behind his desk.

"I presume you advertise your business on television?" After Mariah gave a puzzled affirmative nod, he went on, "My mother gets a little carried away with TV advertising. She orders the most outlandish things. I've considered having her telephone calling restricted, but in her more lucid moments she gets a great deal of joy from calling her friends and relatives. I'm certainly not going to take that away from her even if means paying for a miniature trampoline, cutlery, or a set of records that sound as if they were recorded under a blanket by someone who couldn't carry a tune in a bucket."

"Do you mean my Mrs. Wilson is your mother?" Mariah asked, her eyes widening.

"That's right," the judge admitted. "And you showed yourself to be a good judge of character when you said she was a lovely woman. She'd be mortified if she ever had any idea of the problems she's caused you. What is her debt to you?" he asked with his pen poised over his checkbook. "I insist on making it good."

After Mariah quickly calculated the cost of the unsold tickets, he wrote out a check and handed it to her. Mariah noticed that it was for fifty dollars more than the sum she had named.

"I included a little extra for your time on my mother's behalf, Ms. Benedict, because I know you must charge for your services. I'd like to reimburse you for your time tonight, but I'm afraid that might be considered a little unethical in the eyes of some sticklers who insist on following the letter of the law. Technically, the law considers what you were doing scalping tickets, although we certainly know there were extenuating circumstances. Of course, all charges against you will be dropped and there will be no record with your name on file, I assure you. It's the very least I can do."

Politely ushering Mariah and David from his chambers, the judge laughingly remarked, "My mother always liked a good time. Maybe, if she's feeling well enough, I'll take her to the next rock concert that comes to town. Ms. Benedict, I'd like to hire you to inform me when that is, and to buy the tickets for me—but not until I've given you the money first!"

After a stunned Mariah had accepted the repeated advice of the kindly judge not to make any more major purchases on the basis of phone calls from unfamiliar prospective clients, she and David left the building.

As they stepped out into the night, Mariah noticed it was no longer raining. The dark clouds had started to lift and a few distant stars twinkled through. When they reached the parking lot Mariah threw herself into David's arms.

"Oh, David," she breathed in deeply as though savoring the air around them, "for the first time in my whole life I think I really appreciate what it means to be a free woman!"

Lifting her from the ground, David held her to him as he twirled her completely around before setting her back on her feet.

"I began to suspect there was some connection between the judge and your Mrs. Wilson, as you call her," David said, "almost as soon as you mentioned the name of the nursing home. But Wilson is such a common name that I just couldn't let myself believe it. It seemed too good to be true."

"I know what you mean! It was just as if my nightmare turned into a dream. What a learning experience this has been."

Exhilarated, she slipped her arms around David's strong neck and rewarded him with a passionate kiss. It was long past midnight and she knew that he had had little if any sleep.

"I'm sorry I had to call you out tonight," she said contritely. "But it is so wonderful having you as my best friend."

"Best friend?" David inquired, raising his eyebrows, as he shut the passenger door behind her.

Before he could get into the truck, Mariah jumped out on the driver's side and blocked him.

"Hey!" David remarked with a teasing grin. "Have you grown so fond of this place that you've changed your mind and want to stay?"

"Not on your life!" Mariah replied with an answering smile.

Encircling his waist with her arms, she pulled him to her, her moist pink mouth open and ready for his kiss. She shivered in the warm night air as his lips fell hungrily on hers. At first tender, they soon became more demanding, sending a rush of desire throughout her body. She responded fully, deeply invading his mouth with her tongue, reveling in the groan that rose in his throat. After several long moments in David's sensual embrace, Mariah felt his lips withdraw from hers.

In a ragged voice, hoarse with emotion, David whispered as he lifted her back onto the seat of the truck, "We'd better get out of here before we're arrested for an indecent display of affection in the parking lot of the city jail."

"I just wanted to show you what kind of a friend I thought you were," Mariah purred within the tight circle of his arm as they drove toward the coliseum parking lot so she could pick up her car. "I didn't want to leave you with any mistaken ideas."

CHAPTER NINE

Once the door of Mariah's apartment closed soundly behind them, David took her in his arms. Just being alone together seemed a privilege to them now, and there was a special honeyed sweetness in the kiss they shared.

Feeling David's passions mount, Mariah broke free of the embrace. "I'm sorry, darling, but I have to shower. I feel so dirty after being in that jail cell." A shudder shook her frame at the memory.

"Let me help," he murmured against her hair, his hand moving down her body to unzip her jeans.

"I'd rather do that myself this time. I feel like I have grime in every pore," Mariah said, putting her hand over his. "Just give me a few minutes. Besides, I don't trust you. With your help I may never get to the shower."

Kissing him lightly on the tip of his nose, she added, "You get the bed pulled out, friend, and I'll be with you before you get the pillows on it."

Ignoring her suggestion, David persisted in loosening her clothing as she determinedly inched their entwined bodies closer to the bathroom. When at last she felt the door handle pressing against her hip, she dropped her hands from his shoulders and reached behind her body to turn the knob.

Raising her hands to press against the broad expanse of his chest, she pushed David away. With a mock look of hurt on his face he gave her one more kiss before letting her slide from his arms. As she finished undressing, he turned on the shower water and adjusted the temperature before gathering her naked body to his once more.

"Hurry," he whispered against her lips before he left the small room.

Although she'd intended to do just that, once she was alone in the steamy cubicle, Mariah couldn't get enough of the feel of the hot water streaming against her skin. The odors of her cellmates, the drunken stench of the older woman and the sickening musky scent of the other two's overpowering perfume, seemed to cling to her. No matter how she scrubbed they just wouldn't seem to go away. And even though her fingers appeared clean of the ink that had been placed on them to obtain a good print, she was sure she could still see minute traces of it caught in the curving ridged design of her fingertips. She stayed in the shower, letting its pleasing roar drown out the disquieting thoughts that had begun to trouble her, until the water began to grow decidedly cooler.

Hurriedly turning off the faucet, she stepped from the shower. Careful to avoid the small heap of clothing she'd discarded on the floor, she knew only her thrifty nature would keep her from burning every garment she'd worn while she was in jail. She took time just to towel off the excess moisture from her dripping skin before running out to where David solicitously held the covers up, ready to warm her chilled body with the heat of his when she scrambled in beside him.

Nestled against him, her head resting on his shoulder, Mariah said, "Thanks for being so patient."

"No problem." He gently kissed the top of her damp hair. "I got the message that you needed some time alone."

"When I think about it, David, I really can't understand why I got as upset as I did tonight."

"What are you talking about? Anyone would have been upset under those circumstances. It's not every day a person gets arrested."

"Thank goodness!" Mariah interjected vehemently. "But that's not really what I mean. It made sense for me to be upset about that and for me to worry about what the consequences of being caught scalping would be. When I think about it, it was my reactions to the people around me that I can't understand."

"Such as?" David asked.

"Well, I've known a lot of policemen. When I was working as a cocktail waitress some of them would stop by to have a beer when they got off their shifts. And I've even had to call on-duty ones from time to time when one of the customers had had too much to drink and just wouldn't call it a night."

"So?"

"So, they seemed so different from the ones I met tonight, right from the one who arrested me on. Tonight they all seemed callous and indifferent. The ones I've met in the past seemed like real nice guys."

David chuckled. "They thought you were on the other side of the law tonight, honey. I'd never met a state patrolman I didn't like until the one who pulled me over and told me he'd clocked me going seventy in a fifty-five-mile zone. The taxpayers don't pay cops to be chummy with lawbreakers."

"I guess I was being paranoid," Mariah admitted, feeling a little more comfortable. "They didn't mistreat me."

"Of course they didn't," David agreed. "For a few hours you just got caught up in the system." He attempted to draw her into an embrace, but when Mariah avoided his seeking mouth, suppressing a sigh, he settled back to listen. He would be patient, seeing how important it was for her to resolve her feelings.

"But it was more than that," Mariah continued. "It was the way I felt toward the women in the holding tank with me. I behaved as though I were afraid of them. That was ridiculous. I'm a grown woman with plenty of experience. I'd like to have a dollar for every time I've served an alcoholic beverage, or smelled alcohol on someone's breath. That older lady being drunk shouldn't have been so shocking to me. And those two young women. I've seen dozens like them through the years, especially when I first started working and had to take jobs in lounges that weren't too selective about their clientele.

"I was afraid of them, David." She turned to face him, her eyes full of the distress she felt. "I really was."

Realizing how disturbed she was, David decided to be bluntly frank. "I'm sure you were. And you had reason to be. They were threatening your self-esteem. Even though you encountered women like them before, you were never one of them. When you met their types while you were working as a cocktail

126

waitress, that didn't mean you had anything in common with them. But tonight, when you were thrown together in the same cell, it seemed to you that you were being lumped with them. And, of course through a mistake, you were.

"You felt threatened tonight, Mariah, by the possible loss of your good name and even your freedom. When anyone thinks they're about to lose something they value that much, they're bound to behave a little irrationally. That's all you did, honey. You acted like a normal human being. And you know what else?"

She shook her head, looking up at him with searching eyes.

"I'm damned proud of you. Even though you were having all those feelings, you didn't let it show. You held your head high, and you spoke out, 'not guilty,' loud and clear."

"I did, didn't I?" Mariah remembered. Relaxing, she broke into a smile and pulled the ruffle-edged sheets under her chin. "You've got it all figured out, haven't you?" she teased. "I'll bet you like to think a big, brave guy like you never gets thrown by his emotions." Turning in his arms, she pressed her damp body along the length of his, sliding her arms around his waist and pulling his hips tightly against hers.

"I might like to think that," David admitted with a grin, "but you know all it takes is a feather-weight woman like you to get my emotions all riled up." When Mariah raised her head to playfully nip at his earlobe he let out a moan of delight and pulled her closer.

"Oh, David," she whispered into the golden hair on his chest, "I was so worried about you."

What next? he asked inwardly, hoping that this time the beautiful golden-haired woman could be distracted from any more serious discussion. His fingers tangled in her damp hair, arching back her head. His lips brushed hers as he dutifully asked, "Why?"

"I worried that you might get into an accident driving down to the . . . jail." Mariah shuddered.

"Why would I do that?" he asked dreamily, his tongue slowly circling the raised outline of her lips, enticing her tongue to touch his.

"I was afraid you'd be in the hospital . . ."

His teasing mouth closed over hers, silencing her unspoken fears. For a long moment she was lost in the sweetness of his kiss, grateful that he was in her arms, safe from her imagined terrors. She responded with an intensity of feeling that had been deepening throughout the days and nights she had known him.

His hands left her hair, settled on her shoulders, then slid down her supple back to her buttocks, cupping each swell in his large hands. His tongue invaded the depths of her mouth as though seeking to find every tantalizing pleasure its recesses might hold.

Melded against his feverish body, her lips locked to his, Mariah surrendered herself totally to the love and passion she felt for this sensitive yet commanding man. He had only to touch her and her body responded sensually. He had only to speak and her senses were aroused. Every thought of him warmed her to desire. Now held in the strength of his powerful arms, cradled tightly against the evidence of his desire for her, she was as fluid and unresisting as warm putty.

His lips finally broke from hers, his breathing hoarse and deep.

"Oh, David," Mariah murmured, her voice breathless, still haunted by the fear that she might have lost him.

His hands slid to her armpits, forcing her pliant body from his only long enough to blaze a trail of fiery kisses down her throat to her aching breasts.

"I don't know what you're talking about," David panted, his breath hot against her tender flesh.

Arching her body toward his, she gasped, "I'm glad you're not in the hospital."

"Me too," he agreed fervently, not the least interested in further explanation. As he slid his hand between her thighs, his tongue ravenously circled and teased her erect nipples.

His possessive touch sent her reeling in a spasm of pleasure so electrifying she was sure her heart had stopped in the middle of its thunderous pounding. Surge after surge of shuddering ecstasy shook her frame until she thought she might faint from the torturous pleasure.

Suspended above the rational world on a cloud of exhilarating emotion, she moaned the only thought her mind still held, "I love you so much."

Then, just before his mouth covered hers, she heard him murmur, in a voice deep and torn with rapture, "I love you too, Mariah."

Or was it an echo of her own voice? she wondered as his hot tongue invaded her mouth just as his entry infused her being. Then she no longer knew about or cared for anything other than the supreme enchantment transporting them to a new plane where only pure sensation existed.

How long they stayed there joined in mutual passion, Mariah didn't know. She only knew that after a long while, David's body shuddered spasmodically then sank to hers for a brief moment until he rolled on his side, taking her with him to rest in the wonderful protection of his arms.

Mariah woke from a deep sleep to the twittering of birds in the large elm outside her balcony. Dawn was breaking, lighting up the room with a soft glow. Smiling, she gently kissed the closed lids of David's eyes, reluctant to awaken him although longing for his company.

But at her touch his eyes opened, his endearing gaze searching her face with the love he'd declared as he'd held her body fused to his during their long, wondrous lovemaking. It was, she thought, as if their mutual declarations had added a depth, a new dimension to their relationship, introducing a wild exciting abandon that had left them greatly satisfied with a newer and truer meaning of love.

With a sigh, she sank back against him on the apricot-colored sheet, letting her hands tangle in his thick shock of sun-bleached hair, pulling his face against the swell of her breast. As his mouth found and gently teased erect a rosy nipple, Mariah sighed again with contentment.

"What's all that sighing about?" David asked, finding and giving the other nipple its fair share of attention.

"I just wish you didn't have to go to work so early this morning. I don't think I could bear to have you

130

leave. And you haven't had much sleep." She laughed, remembering the kaleidoscope of events that had kept him from a peaceful night's rest. It had been a night to remember, in more ways than one.

"I don't have to go to the site this morning. Even though we didn't take the boat trip, I took a few days off."

"I've felt so guilty about that," Mariah admitted. "You'll never know how badly I wished we had been on the open seas when I was in that cell last night."

"I can imagine," David said dryly. "At that point I'll bet even the prospect of seasickness and my company looked good."

"David!" Mariah protested his tease. Rising above him, she lightly covered his face with her down pillow before lifting it away. "You know I wanted to go with you. You should have gone by yourself, even if I did have to take care of those damned tickets."

"And missed all the fun?" He grinned. "Not on your life. Besides, what would you have done if you hadn't had me to call?"

"You've got a point there," Mariah admitted, a rueful smile lighting her gray eyes. "I suppose I would have thrown myself on the mercy of the court. Not intentionally, you understand, but because my knees would have buckled on my way to the bench."

"I doubt that." David returned her smile. "But I'm glad I was there, nevertheless.

"So, I'm staying home this morning and you've got me in bed. Just what did you have in mind?" His mock leer was just short of successful.

"After last night, I wouldn't need three chances to guess what you have on yours!" Mariah teased. Grinning with pure contentment, she feathered kisses

131

down the side of his slightly stubbly cheek and neck before putting her head down on the pillow once more. Snaking a hand under the covers she carefully brought it to rest on his flat abdomen, just below his navel.

"And you're trying to say you have something different in mind, you insatiable little witch?" David asked, bringing to bear all the self-restraint he possessed.

"Well," Mariah murmured, "I was just worried about this." She gently patted his abdomen and ruffed up his descending line of virile hair with her fingertips.

"About what?" David asked. Pulling her to face him he caught her meandering hand in his.

"About your stomach, silly," she replied, her eyes wide with feigned innocence. "I thought you must be terribly hungry by now. For one thing, I don't think you had any dinner last night, did you? I thought I'd fix breakfast and serve it to you in bed."

"Now that's a nice wifely thought," David remarked with approval, and her heart soared at the word. "But, sweetie, I think you have a little to learn about anatomy." Taking her hand he placed it just below the center of his rib cage. "For further reference, my stomach," he emphasized the word, "is here."

"Really," Mariah remarked, her eyes sparkling wickedly.

"Really," he replied with a grin. Bending his head to catch an upturned nipple between his teeth, he added, "And if you're even slightly serious about this breakfast in bed business, you'd better get started before you end up being the main course."

"Whatever you say, darling." Mariah started to swing her legs from the bed.

"Just a second," David said. Reaching out, his hand gently circled her upper arms, pulling her back down beside him. "While we're on this subject, we have some things we might as well settle now."

"What things?" she asked dreamily, snuggling up to him.

"First of all about your business. Now that you've made it a fact of life for many people in the community you can sell it. You shouldn't have any trouble at all with your track record. You've got a name, a service and an established clientele to sell. That should be worth quite a bit."

"Why would I want to do that?"

"Because it's beginning to interfere with us," David explained, growing more impatient every second. "After last night you should be able to understand that."

"I do, David. Really, I do. I won't take any more night work after this week," she promised. "I'll keep it strictly nine to five."

"How about this winter when we go to Hawaii?" he asked suspiciously.

"I thought you'd never ask!" she squealed, sitting up slightly to kiss the top of his head. "I've already thought about hiring and training an assistant. I felt awful about turning you down about the boat trip. You needed the vacation. I made a promise to myself to never let that happen again."

"Ms. Efficiency!" David pronounced, finding himself filled with admiration for this woman. "You've got an answer for everything!"

"I hope so, David," Mariah answered earnestly. "I

don't want anything to ever come between us, but I love my work. I love having a real career that I can make grow and shape with my own initiative. I love the respect I get from my clients. Believe me, that's new for me. And I especially like working for myself."

"I can understand what you're saying, Mariah, but I've worked hard to get where I am too," David stated in a firm voice. "And I did it with one thought in mind—to be financially independent and to provide a good living for my wife and family. After we're married, you won't need to work. You can volunteer —get involved in community affairs. But you won't have to be at anyone else's beck and call."

"David, that's not fair! I just explained that I want a career. I wouldn't dream of asking you to give up your job. Don't you think I have as much right to mine?"

"You've got me there," he admitted. "I'll have to think about it. Right now all I'm interested in is that breakfast."

Mariah hummed happily as she whipped up the Belgium waffle mixture and poured it into the heated iron. Her mind was filled with plans for the future—a future as Mrs. David Anthony. "Mariah Anthony," she tried out the sound of her new name to be under her breath. It couldn't be more perfect. Perhaps they'd get married in Hawaii! What a wonderful place for a honeymoon.

But David, lying on the daybed, was more than a little worried. That he wanted Mariah was not in doubt—it was her career he could do without. It had turned out to be far too engrossing and time-consuming. He wanted Mariah's time to be centered around their life together—not her business.

How had he let things go so far? he wondered, gently rubbing the stubble of his blond beard. Financing her little venture had seemed like such a small thing. In his mind, he realized, he had seen it as an opportunity to give her something to do until they could really get to know each other. If things hadn't worked out between them, Mariah's success or failure would have been inconsequential. Such a minor amount of money had been involved that he could have written it off without a qualm.

But she had made a go of it, and he had fallen in love with her. So now he was faced with a dilemma of another sort, one he had never predicted, and certainly couldn't write off.

Grudgingly, he had to admit, as he heard the sound of the blender humming in the kitchenette, that her business success had added to the depth of the love he felt for her. She was an admirable woman. His initial fascination with her as an incredibly attractive woman had matured and ripened to a deep love as he'd watched her staunchly face up to countless problems in her successful struggle to make her business viable.

His eyes lit with a special pleasure as she entered the room, her outstretched arms carrying breakfast trays for them both.

"How the hell can you keep both of those things balanced?" he asked as she expertly set his before him, then placed hers on the bed and seated herself cross-legged beside him.

"I was a waitress. Did you forget?" she asked with a pert smile.

"As a matter of fact I did for a minute. This is delicious," he said as he finished a bite of the thick waffle topped with strawberries and whipped cream. "You can give the cook my compliments."

"Thank you, sir, I'll pass that along, but frankly I'm more interested in my tip!" Mariah said happily.

As they sat in bed with their breakfast trays, able to laugh about Mariah's jail cell experiences in the light of day, there was no trace in Mariah's banter that she had any concern about the conflict David feared needed to be faced soon. Perhaps, he allowed himself to hope, once the idea of being his wife had had time to sink in, she'd consider being married career enough to satisfy her.

When they'd finished their leisurely breakfast, Mariah cleared away the dishes while David showered. She smiled hearing him whistling slightly off key, and she nearly felt like a married woman as he helped her make the bed and straighten up the small apartment before they dressed. Watching him, enjoying the masculine beauty of his every move, she was glad David had let the question of her career drop so easily. Maybe too easily, she thought for a moment before slipping on her shoes. No, I'm seeing trouble where there isn't any, she reasoned, scoffing at her suspicious thought. If he really objected he would be forthright enough to tell her. He wasn't the kind of man to hold anything back. He was the most honest person she'd ever met.

Contentment filled her as they got ready for the day and kissed good-bye at the sidewalk. She watched him as he piled into his truck and drove off, before she started her Supra. David had said he needed to take care of a little paperwork, even

136

though he was still officially on vacation. Mariah took satisfaction in each of them going off to face the day at their separate jobs, remembering with pleasure David's promise that he'd be home early and that they'd go out for dinner.

Perhaps, she allowed herself to dream, perhaps tonight he would formally propose and she'd accept. How she'd love to be wearing a diamond engagement ring tomorrow. No matter how small the stone, she knew that if David gave it to her, its brilliance would outdazzle anything she had ever seen or imagined.

CHAPTER TEN

That noon, Mariah didn't know as she sat at a booth with Jeff Holden and animatedly related her experiences at night court, that David, after seeing her car parked outside the restaurant he knew she frequently stopped at for lunch, had decided to join her. She didn't see the look of fury that appeared on his face when his gaze alighted on the two of them laughing uproariously across the room from where he stood. Nor did she know the suspicions that clouded the rest of David's day as he jealously tried to figure out the true nature of Mariah and Jeff's relationship . . . and just where, if anywhere, his own relationship with Mariah was heading.

Mariah couldn't know how profoundly the chance encounter would affect David's passion-scarred heart, making him wonder whether he really knew the woman he'd at last allowed himself to love and trust, couldn't know that to David, who had wanted to resume their half-finished talk, it seemed as though Mariah were constantly creating more obstacles between them just when he was trying to sort things out and reach a resolution. David began to think their problems might be insurmountable. And he began to wonder if the effort of trying to work things out between them was worth the emotional trauma that would result if he ultimately failed and lost her.

Deep hurt goaded David into irrationality as he thought of and magnified in importance the times Jeff had played joker in the past.

The evening Mariah had looked forward to with such joy and hope was not a success. David, though polite, was quiet. Mariah initiated what she hoped would be a lively conversation, but when he sat aloof and didn't bother to make an effort to hold up his end, she finally gave up. Unshed tears stung her eyes as she covered his hand with hers. This was the date she'd looked forward to all day, the date she had imagined would end with their being officially engaged. She rubbed the conspicuously bare third finger of her left hand where she'd hoped he would place an engagement ring while making declarations of undying love.

"Did you have a bad day?" she ventured.

"No." His answer was abrupt, effectively squelching any further attempt at communication between them.

Taking her hand from his, Mariah picked up her fork and started on her salad with a lack of interest she found difficult to conceal. Was David having second thoughts about telling her he loved her? she contemplated fearfully. Was last night, the night of her deepest commitment to anyone, to be merely a memory? When the waitress served their meals, looking down at her plate of beautifully prepared food, Mariah felt like gagging.

139

* * *

Slipping out of bed so as not to awaken David, Mariah walked out to her balcony and sank dejectedly into the bright yellow captain's chair. Remembering the first time she and David had sat there together at the beginning of summer, the tears she had been willfully holding back all evening spilled over and ran unheeded down her cheeks.

After the bust of a dinner, David's lovemaking had been perfunctory, almost mechanical. It had been as if she'd forced him into it by pushing herself close and kissing his cradled head. She had hoped that after they got in bed he would tell her what was wrong. But when she'd gathered the courage to ask, him what was bothering him, he'd replied with the unsatisfactory word "Nothing."

Seeing this obstinate side of him for the first time and realizing the ability he had to hurt her through withdrawal and silence, Mariah was deeply worried.

Searching her mind for a reason to account for his behavior, the only thing she could dredge up that might be bothering him—other than her nagging fear that he'd come to the conclusion she was simply the wrong woman for him—was his conviction that she should sell her business because it absorbed too much of her attention. Paradoxically, if she'd agreed to do that, just where would she be in the future if their paths parted?

Hating herself for doubting his love yet unable to quiet her fears, Mariah sat disconsolately until the cool and dampness of the night drove her back to bed.

The next evening, after deliberately fixing David's favorite foods in an effort to show him how much she cared, Mariah found his mood as impenetrable as the evening before. She decided to face him down until he confided what his problem was, knowing she couldn't go to bed with him again until she got to the bottom of his mood. If he was sorry that in a moment of passion he had said more than he'd intended, she wanted to know, even though it would cause her more pain than his disinterest. But to her dismay, just as she was about to question him, her beeper sounded. After getting the message, she placed a call.

"Well, I am in the middle of dinner . . . Yes, Mr. Rosenthal, I can understand that your wife needs to get out of the house . . . Certainly." Mariah glanced nervously at David, who had not lifted his eyes from his plate. "Oh, is she a little depressed? I'm sorry to hear that." Mariah suppressed a sigh. "Of course I'll go . . . That's right, just meet me in line ten minutes before the doors are due to open . . . Well, I hope this cheers her up too. I'll see you then."

Placing the phone in its cradle, she returned to the table to remove her plate of barely touched food.

"I'm sorry, but I have to go out. That was Mr. Rosenthal, the older gentleman whose wife is confined to a wheelchair. She's a little down and he thinks attending the premiere at the State Theater of a new movie will cheer her up. I'll have to hurry to get downtown in that line. Will you be all right?" Mariah asked, though the question sounded silly to her own ears. She just felt so awkward around David when he was like this that she didn't know what to say.

"Of course, aren't I always?" His question was terse, and she knew he didn't expect a reply.

Arriving at the theater, Mariah was pleasantly surprised to see Jeff Holden there. When he motioned her to take a place in front of him, Mariah quickly responded to his offer even though she ordinarily disliked people who cut lines. Tonight she didn't care what the people behind them thought. All that was important was knowing that the moments saved would hasten her return to David.

"Mariah, I'd like you to meet Ginny Matthews," Jeff said as he introduced her to an attractive brunette.

Catching an air of possessiveness in Jeff's manner toward the young woman, Mariah began to wonder if this was more than a casual date. As they chatted and she learned that Jeff was managing the estate left to Ginny by her late husband, Mariah's suspicions that Jeff had at long last met his match in the charming woman crystallized into certainty. Jeff had the unmistakable look of a man in love. The look she'd seen in David's eyes less than forty-eight hours before.

Suddenly Mariah felt a stab of pain. Why hadn't she asked David if he wanted to see the show? She had been so preoccupied with her determination to get to the bottom of his problem that she hadn't even thought of it. Instead she'd left him alone and run out!

Feeling contrite and guilty, she asked, "Jeff, would you hold my place while I call David and ask him if he'd like to see the show? I should have thought of it before."

"Sure thing," Jeff readily answered. "It's time for

Ginny and David to meet. I want the four of us to be friends."

Mariah managed a smile though she wasn't nearly as certain as Jeff at the moment of her future as one of the foursome.

After dialing the number of her apartment she let the phone ring an absurd number of times before she hung up and repeated the same futile procedure at David's apartment. Hanging up, she forlornly took the quarter from the metal cup and absently dropped it into her handbag, pasting a smile on her face before returning to the line.

Driven by brooding jealousy, David wheeled his sleek black Jaguar from the garage below his apartment building for the first time in months. He snorted. How ridiculous it had been to hide the expensive car from Mariah. If he had any sense he would have been driving her around in it all summer, enjoying the way her golden blondness would complement the sleek lines of the powerful machine. What a fool he'd been! A first-class, first-cabin fool, he had to give himself that. No one could have made a bigger ass of himself.

Keeping up the front that he was an ordinary working man until he was certain of her love for him had been a fantasy. Yet on the other hand, maybe it hadn't been such a bad idea. Just when he'd become sure she was the right woman for him, and had declared his love for her, he'd found out that she was seeing Jeff Holden behind his back. Had that been going on all along? Had there been a logical reason for their meeting? He had no idea, having been too proud to question her.

One thing was for sure, though, when he got to that theater she had better be there, he thought grimly, or it would be all over between them. But even as he silently voiced the ultimatum, pain gripped his heart. How could he give up the most wonderful woman he'd ever met? How could he live without her love and caring?

Allowing jealousy to make a fool of him once more, unable to keep himself from deliberately repeating the degrading lunchtime scene of spying on the woman he loved, David drove to the theater and parked his car at the end of the full lot. Keeping himself a few rows of cars back from the line, he walked along until he spotted Mariah's long fall of golden hair. Then his heart skipped a beat when he saw Jeff Holden standing right behind her. What more proof could he have? Leaving him sitting home with a casserole of potatoes whatever, while she met another man!

Stalking rapidly to his car, he simultaneously slammed the door and started the engine. Jamming it into gear, with tires squealing, he raced it out of the parking lot.

When Mariah returned to her apartment after giving up her place in line to the Rosenthals, she found the food she'd left David still setting untouched on his plate. It hadn't come as a surprise that he wasn't there since he hadn't answered her call. As soon as she'd driven up she'd noticed that his truck wasn't parked in front of the building. But nevertheless she'd gone up to her apartment hoping he'd left a note.

Finding none, she immediately locked her door and drove to David's apartment resolved to finish what she'd set out to do. Torn between anguish and anger, Mariah knew that unless things were settled between them soon, there would be no way they could recapture the idyllic moments of their love—hurt and suspicion would take their toll, and she loved David Anthony too much to allow that to happen.

Mariah pulled into a spot reserved for visitors in front of the building where David lived. It was odd, she thought, feeling suddenly uncomfortable, that even though David had a key to her place and came and went as he pleased, she could count the number of times she'd been to his apartment on one hand. They'd just spent one night there, and the other times they'd stayed only a few minutes while he stopped by to pick up some clothes. He'd told her that he preferred her place, because her personality was reflected in every corner of it.

It was true, she thought as she walked up the sidewalk, that David's apartment was furnished with only the basics. When she'd looked around the night she'd stayed there, the only clue to the personality or occupation of its male inhabitant had been bookcases filled with construction and code manuals, as well as books containing plans for multi-family dwellings.

Standing outside his door, she couldn't bring herself to knock. Instead she tried the door handle and to her great relief it was unlocked. Once inside, she crossed through the entryway, heading in the direction of the light and noise coming from the living room.

"David, I called you from the theater, but you didn't answer. After I got there I wondered if maybe you'd have liked to see the movie. I'm sorry I ran out without asking you," Mariah explained to the man sprawled in front of the TV in the good-sized room. "I just didn't take time to think." It hadn't escaped her that he'd neither stood nor acknowledged her presence after she'd let herself into his apartment.

"I went to the theater. Didn't you get enough of Holden at lunch yesterday? Was it necessary for you to run out to see him this evening too?" His accusing tone was as heavy as a lead weight dropped on her heart.

Mariah felt the blood rush to her face as the meaning of his accusation sank in. "If you saw me standing with Jeff tonight," she said quietly, "are you so blind that you didn't see the lovely brunette who was with him? Jeff offered me a place in line and I took it so I could get back to you that much earlier. And yesterday I had lunch with Jeff after I'd made my loan payment with the judge's check. If you saw us, why didn't you join us?"

"Two's company, three's a crowd."

"What's that supposed to mean? That there's only to be the two of us and no one else will be allowed in our lives? What if we have children? Will that be a crowd you don't feel you belong in?"

"There won't be any children if you date other men behind my back!"

"David, you're talking to Mariah Benedict not Carla whatever-her-name-is! Just because you got stung once doesn't mean that every woman is out to poison your happiness. You've got to remove the stinger Carla left festering in you before you're going to be able to love again without pain. And I think you're the only one who can do that.

"I love you and only you. Does that mean I have to

quit my job and wear a black veil when I go out on the street? So I won't run into or be recognized by anyone I know, because you might see me talking to a man and jump to the conclusion that there was something between us?"

"Don't be ridiculous," David snarled. "Carla has nothing to do with you and me. I know how Jeff works. But I thought you were above that sort of thing."

"What sort of thing? I owe Jeff some consideration. I know that the bank didn't lend me the money for my business. Jeff did it out of friendship to you. And if I have lunch with him, why does that threaten you?"

"Jeff didn't lend you that money," David exploded, feeling the red heat of jealousy rise behind his eyes. "I did! And if I'd had any idea how much your hare-brained scheme was going to upset our lives, I'd never have done it."

Stunned into angry silence by his disclosure, Mariah sat with an audible plop on the black leather couch, her quick mind trying to process all the infor-mation it had just received.

"Harebrained scheme?" she challenged. "As I re-call you were right in there every minute with your suggestions for PCs and logos and all those other things I'd never heard of. You were sure hot for the idea in June."

"I wanted to make sure you didn't have to go back to the cocktail scene. I couldn't stand the idea of other men ogling you and making drunken passes at you."

"It bothered you enough that you'd take a risk the bank wouldn't? How could you do that? Where did you get that much money? I don't want your savings.

How are you going to live in the winter if you gave me your money?

"Or," she went on, her mouth voicing the thoughts her teeming brain busily concocted, "did you think you could buy me? That first day I met you, you shoved money into my hand. Do you think you can buy what you want and keep it on a shelf?

"I can see now that you're so jealous nothing else matters. You're willing to destroy your own happiness. You think you own me, don't you?"

Standing abruptly, Mariah nearly fell back onto the couch. Regaining her dignity, she shouted out at the silent man who had stood up and was walking toward her, his arms raised to grasp her arms.

"Don't you touch me! I'm going to the bank in the morning to get a real loan. I'll pay you back every red cent with interest! In fact, since you think Jeff is so fascinating, maybe I will start dating him." Mariah had intended to tell David her happy suspicions concerning Jeff and Ginny, but she decided he could find that out later on his own. Right now she was just interested in getting her hands on any weapon that could hurt David as badly as she'd been hurt. And knowing David's weakness, Jeff was it. "There must be something there I've overlooked since you seem to think he's such a great lover! At least if I were going with him he'd take me out on a date once in a while which is more than I can say for the arrangement I've had with you!"

She stalked toward the door. Then turning back, she added, "And as for my job interfering with our relationship, how about yours? You work from sunup to sundown, leaving precious few hours for me. I never complained about that. In fact, other than the exception of the boat trip, I've done everything I could to arrange my hours around yours!" Angrily she threw open the door.

"Mariah, you're not leaving until you listen to me." David took a few steps toward her.

"Like hell I'm not. I waited for two days to hear what was bothering you. Talking to you has been like banging my head against a brick wall. Now that I find out how childishly you've been acting, and how you've deceived me . . . and spied on me! I don't give a damn!"

Mariah ran from the apartment. Blinded by tears, she drove slowly home and flung herself on the couch. She stirred only long enough to angrily detach her ringing phone from the jack. Then quickly she opened her radio page and shook out the batteries. David Anthony wasn't going to get in his two cents! He'd already said too much. She sobbed as she fell back on the couch muffling her tears in a pillow.

The rest of the week was agony. Mariah had never known the anguish of a breaking heart and the emotional pain seemed far worse than any physical discomfort she'd ever suffered. How long would it last? she wondered bleakly. Was there a prescribed length of time it took for a heart to heal?

When she thought over the few details David had told her about his break with Carla, she knew that her suspicions that he'd been crippled by it were true. Obviously he was afraid to love again unless he could build a protective wall around the object of his love.

But she was not an object, she reminded herself. And she couldn't be loved jealously. She had to be free to give her love. She couldn't live her life under suspicion, no matter how much she loved him.

She didn't go to the bank to get her loan refinanced. She was afraid to go near Jeff Holden, not because of what her feelings were toward him, but because somehow she felt it would be a betrayal of David in his friend's eyes. And though part of her was determined never to see David again, her heart longed for things between them to return to the way they were when they'd been so blissfully happy.

David's mood was black. It seemed as though the light and color had gone out of his life when Mariah walked out on him. No matter how many times he reran the scene of their argument in his mind he couldn't understand what had made her so angry. He'd been on the verge of confessing everything to her: his actual status as owner of Superior Construction Company, his decision to retire from actively working as a carpenter on his job sites, and his hopes and dreams for their marriage and life together. But she'd become so damned angry she hadn't given him a chance. Good thing he hadn't said any more. She'd gotten mad enough when she'd found out that he hadn't leveled with her over the bank loan, how would she have reacted if he'd dumped the whole load on her at once?

Actually she should be grateful to him for lending her the money, he rationalized. How many times had she said how grateful she was to Jeff and to the bank for giving her a start? Now that she knew the truth, why wasn't she grateful to him? It just didn't make any sense.

Mariah's parting shot that she might start dating

Jeff was the one that rankled most. He was fairly sure now that her relationship with Jeff had been innocent—at least from her point of view. Jeff? Now that was another story altogether. For all he knew Jeff might have set his sights on Mariah right from the start. Obviously Jeff was getting all the mileage he could out of Mariah's gratitude.

Though he despised himself for it, David had spent a part of every night parked down the street from Mariah's building, unrecognized in the black Jag, and he knew that so far, she'd come home alone. He wasn't proud of his actions, but he was so damned jealous he couldn't help himself, just as he couldn't help dwelling on the meaning of Jeff and Mariah's midday meetings. Had he been like this before Carla? he wondered miserably. Not that he could remember.

Mariah. Mariah was the one person in the world who could help him out of this almost suffocating jealousy. Mariah could cure him of this affliction. As things stood now he was jealous of anything and everything that came between them. When you got right down to it, that was his real objection to her career. It took too much of her time.

And he wanted her time and attention. It was all he could do to keep from accosting her on the street and bodily carrying her up to her apartment. He needed to be alone with her, to talk with her and force her to listen. He'd be waiting in her apartment now, but he'd found out days ago that she'd had the lock changed so that his key no longer fit.

She was so damned mad and so obstinate that nothing he'd tried had had any effect. She'd slammed the phone down in his ear time after time and had insisted that the florist take back every bouquet of flowers he'd sent. The only contact he had had with her was through her answering service and only when she was convinced it was strictly business. It was obvious Mariah needed time to cool off before she'd discuss their personal problems.

Jeff. The more he thought of Jeff, the more his blood boiled. He had a score to settle with that guy, and this time he'd settle it once and for all.

The next day, David picked up the phone.

"Hey, buddy, what do you know?" David asked pleasantly, having decided not to tip his hand.

"Not much. How about you?" Jeff asked.

"Just wondering if you could squeeze me in for lunch?"

"Sure. How does one thirty sound?"

"Fine. I'll meet you at the Palms." Perversely he'd chosen the very restaurant where he'd seen Mariah and Jeff engaged in their cozy conversation.

"Great. See you then."

Irritated with Jeff's cheerful acceptance, David slammed down the receiver. Looking at his watch, he saw he had several hours on his hands before their meeting. Being in no mood to go to the office or the site, he whiled away the time driving around town.

He was parked at the restaurant when Jeff came wheeling up. Jumping from his Jaguar, David purposefully strode over to Jeff's car. As Jeff got out and started to swing his door shut, David reached out and grabbed his shoulder, swinging him around before grasping the lapels of his suit jacket.

"Hey, what do you think you're doing?" Jeff stammered. "I paid five hundred bucks for this suit. Let go of me."

"Stay away from my woman, understand?" David threatened as he loosened his grip.

To David's dismay, after casually adjusting his suit and jutting his chin as he straightened his tie, Jeff laughed.

"Your woman? Mariah? I couldn't get to first base with her if I wanted to. She's so hung up on you she can't talk about anything else. I've taken her to lunch exactly three times and you've been the major topic of conversation." He held up a finger each time he uttered the word, "Boring, boring, boring," to emphasize his point. "That hardly makes me a rival."

"What did she want to know about me, and what did you tell her?"

"Relax. I got the picture from her side. I didn't blow your cover. We're buddies, remember? I don't know what you're pulling with her, but my advice is don't fool around with her too much. She's a bright cookie and she's going to find out who you are one of these days. In fact, that was one reason I agreed to lunch today. As I said, I don't know what games you're playing with her, but if your intentions aren't honorable, as they say in the movies, you're going to have to answer to old Uncle Jeff."

"Uncle Jeff, my foot," David almost shouted. "Lechers don't change their spots."

"Good one," Jeff acknowledged with a maddening grin. "Now put your fists away. We're not college kids anymore, brawling over a broad that neither one of us really wanted. Grownups don't resort to punching it out. Or haven't you noticed? Besides, I don't want blood stains on this suit." Looking down, he brushed away an imaginary bit of lint.

"Come on, I'm hungry," he went on in his suave tones, maddening David further.

But as Jeff strolled toward the green-and-white-canopied entry of the casual restaurant, David fell in step beside him.

After they'd been seated in a booth by a window and each had ordered wine and his meal, Jeff looked intently at David. "What's the matter, having trouble with your love life?"

For a long moment, David looked into Jeff's eyes. Jeff did not avert his gaze.

"Ah, go ahead, tell me about it. I don't know what I can do to help you. But I can listen. It's been a long time since we've sat down and really talked. To tell you the truth I've missed it. You look like a fermented keg ready to explode. Is Mariah playing hard to get?"

Suddenly abandoning his resentment, David grinned. It *had* been a long time since he and Jeff had discussed anything personal. Jeff had been his best friend and, until David had married Carla, there hadn't been anything they hadn't discussed for hours over a couple of beers at the campus watering hole. And except for Jeff's infuriating habit of dating girls David had become interested in, he had been a good friend.

Maybe if he used Jeff as a sounding board, he could get his own thinking straight. He waited to speak until the waitress had set a glass of white wine before each of them. When she left, he took a deep swallow.

"Mariah found out that I was the one who lent her the money and she's madder than hell," David said, watching his friend's face for any sign of amusement.

"Honesty in lending," Jeff intoned with a mock pompousness. "That's been the motto of our bank since it was founded. Any time you screw around with that principle, you've got trouble. I knew from the start that you hadn't thought this deal through. I only went along with it because you're my buddy."

"And you didn't want to lose my account," David promptly reminded him.

"That swayed my judgment somewhat, I do have to admit," Jeff agreed. Relaxing against the padded booth, he slowly swirled the wine in his glass before taking a swallow. "But now that I've come to know Mariah a little better," David noticed with amusement that his friend was careful to emphasize the word "little," "I'm convinced you did the right thing. Your business instincts were right on target as usual. That woman has class and brains. I admire your taste." He raised his half-empty glass in salute.

"You always did," David remarked sarcastically but without rancor.

"Hey, I never interfered with you and Carla. Once I saw how things were between you two, I stayed clear, didn't I?"

"Yeah, and I always wondered why." David leaned forward, tensing slightly, anxious for Jeff's reply.

"Let's just say she wasn't my type and let it go at that."

The two men fell silent as the waitress served their food. As David ate the small salad and crab au gratin he'd ordered, he realized it was the first food he'd been able to taste for days. Perhaps, he thought, Mariah had been right. Perhaps Carla had left him with a festering stinger that only he could remove. Just seeing Jeff and talking to him like this must be

155

part of the process she'd meant he had to go through. Already he felt better.

Pushing the remnants of his club sandwich to the side, Jeff continued where he'd left off, "I'd hate to admit that I could see through Carla from the start. You'd never buy that. She wasn't the right one for you either, obviously. But Mariah is, I'd stake my bottom dollar on that."

"Your dollar is in trouble," David remarked ruefully. "Mariah won't see me, talk to me, or even acknowledge that I'm alive. She still handles our previous business commitments like bank drops and permits, and sets up appointments with contractors and inspectors, but other than that nothing."

"I thought you had a secretary, what was her name?"

"She got married and went on a honeymoon. Mariah helped out during that time. Then when Julie came back she only wanted to work part-time. With Mariah doing all the running around that left Julie with only the telephone and payroll. It worked out really well. Actually saved me money."

"Saved money and lost the woman," Jeff remarked cryptically. "You know, I think we've just come up with a profound maxim."

"Not in Carla's case," David reminded him with a chuckle.

"Back to the drawing board," Jeff conceded with a grin. "So much for profound statements. You know, that's about the first time I can remember you being able to laugh about what happened between you and Carla."

"Well, I'm not laughing about Mariah," David added glumly.

"Boy meets girl, boy loses girl, boy wins girl and they live happily ever after."

"What are you talking about?"

"The course of true love," Jeff remarked sagely. "You're at the second phase. Now what did you say or do to cause this predicament?"

"Well . . . I suggested she sell her business since it was interfering with our lives."

"And?"

"She doesn't want to, and believe me that's an understatement. She says it makes her feel like a worthy person in the business community and she's not about to give it up for any man."

"I can understand that. Why do you want her out of it? Come on, real answers. No rationalizing allowed."

David shrugged, reluctantly forming his reply. "I guess maybe I'm jealous of the time she spends on her job when I have some time off. I asked her to go to the San Juans with me and she said she couldn't because of her weekend commitments."

"She could train an assistant," Jeff suggested.

"She's already thought of that."

"So where's the problem?"

"Well, I really saw red the night I saw her standing in line at the theater with you. I thought that you and she . . . you know."

Jeff let out a hearty laugh. "Saw green, buddy, saw green, not red. Don't you know that half the stuff I've pulled on you with women over the years was because it was so damned much fun and so damned easy to make you jealous? Hell, it didn't matter who the woman was or how little she meant to you. If I showed the slightest interest in her you'd turn pickle green with jealousy.

"But," Jeff added, his expression growing sober, "you'll have to admit I've never given you any problems when I thought the relationship had even a remote chance for the future.

"How did you see Mariah and me? We didn't see you. In fact I held her place in line so she could call you and make it a double date. What were you doing, driving around checking up on her?"

David knew the flush he could feel spreading across his face told Jeff clearer than words that he'd scored a point.

Ignoring his friend's discomfort, Jeff went on. "You know, David, I wasn't joking. I didn't even know half those girls in college you were ready to punch me out for dating. You were always so jealous and ready for a fight that I couldn't resist stirring you up. That's kid stuff, buddy. It's time you grew up and learned to trust your instincts when it comes to women. Jealousy never made the heart grow fonder. In fact, just the opposite.

"I know you got burned by Carla. She led you down the garden path and stole the roses as she went. But Mariah's not Carla. She's already proved that she can and wants to make it on her own. What more do you want?"

"Not another thing," David answered truthfully. Mariah was it. He'd give up everything he'd worked for if he had to for another chance with her.

"Then level with her. What I can't understand is how you've kept her in the dark so far. How've you kept her from finding out who and what you really are?"

158

David let out a deep sigh and pushed his plate away. "I laid down the law to Julie right from the start that she wasn't to let anything slip. She didn't like it, but I made it clear it was one of the terms of her employment."

When Jeff shook his head disgustedly, David said, "I know, I know. I've been a real jerk. I can see that now. As for the rest of it? We've stayed at her place, and besides, only the manager knows I own the complex where I live. I haven't taken her out much, so none of the guys down at the county-city building knows of our personal relationship. I guess nothing's ever happened to come up down there.

"Actually," he admitted sheepishly, "I think I've been hoping for quite some time that she'd find out accidentally so I wouldn't have to tell her."

"I'll give it to you straight, pal," Jeff said. "No sugar coating. You've been dishonest and Mariah doesn't deserve that kind of treatment. From what she tells me, you've been playing the poor working man for all it's been worth. She's even wondering how she can offer you a job with her firm during your down time, but she doesn't know how to do it without quote, undermining your masculinity, unquote."

"She said that?"

"And a lot more. She's crazy about you. Go get her, Tiger. Right now I have to get back to my desk. I've got a two thirty appointment with my fiancée." Jeff threw in the last so casually that David almost thought he hadn't heard right.

"Your fiancée?"

"That's right," Jeff said with a proud smile. "Ginny Matthews. You'd have met her the other night at the movies if you'd bothered to stop and talk for a while.

I told Mariah I wanted the four of us to get together. I hope that's going to happen real soon."

"Well, I'll be damned," David said, shaking his head incredulously.

"Flip for the check?" Jeff asked. Pulling a coin from his pocket, he gestured toward the small white slip the waitress had left on the table when she'd delivered their meal.

"On me this time, as usual," David said with a grin. "For once I feel as if I got my money's worth." Standing, he held out his hand.

"Good," Jeff answered, shaking David's hand, "I'll save my share for your wedding gift."

"That'll be a first," David retorted amiably, glad that their relationship had been restored to its old familiar footing.

"I was your best man," Jeff bantered. "What greater gift than that? Besides, this time I'll have Ginny to pick the gift out and you'll get to keep it. I'll bet Carla made off with all the others."

CHAPTER ELEVEN

David crossed his long legs at the ankle, able to stretch them out now that Jeff no longer sat across the booth from him. A wry smile twisted his lips. Jeff had always been able to raise his spirits, and in spite of the fool he'd made of himself in the parking lot, Jeff had done it again. With his glib tongue and gregarious nature it wasn't hard to understand why Jeff had been able to advance so far in one of the state's largest banks.

But the guy was getting older, David thought glumly. During lunch he had really looked at his college friend and seen the marks that time was engraving on his face. Touching his own hard-planed face and self-consciously feeling under his eyes for any sign of sags, David contemplated that neither he nor Jeff was getting any younger. It was time he got his life in order and started a family.

After ordering another glass of wine from the waitress as she began clearing the dishes away, he leaned back in the blue padded booth mulling over both the wine and his thoughts. Jeff had been right, he realized. For the first time since the divorce, memories of Carla didn't send blood coursing angrily to his head. For years just the mention of Carla was enough to set him off. But today, each time Jeff had spoken her name, the reaction had become less violent until when Jeff joked about the wedding gifts with uncanny accuracy, David had been able to laugh freely with him.

Carla was finished. She no longer held the power to dictate his actions. And Mariah was not Carla, as Jeff had pointed out. She was a warm, loving woman who was able to stand on her own two feet and face the world without pretension or deceit.

Squirming in his seat, David declared himself guilty on both counts: pretension and deceit. When Mariah had openly confided that she was unemployed, he'd let her think he was a day laborer. When she'd revealed her nonexistent bank account, he'd led her to believe that he was nearly as penniless as she was due to the debts Carla had run up long ago.

When Mariah had gone to the bank, he'd allowed her to harbor the illusion that the bank or, worse yet, Jeff had underwritten her loan. David had lived a secluded life with her, keeping the truth about their relationship largely within her own four walls for fear they might meet someone who'd blow his cover.

And now he proposed to tell her it had all been make-believe? That he was really Prince Charming in disguise? That he'd made his first million and had most of it in the bank waiting for the right woman to come along to help him spend it? That he'd built for himself and owned a dozen huge apartment complexes all over town just like the one he was presently finishing? And that now, after observing her closely and living intimately with her for months, he'd made up his mind he could trust her enough to disclose who and what he was?

He let out a self-derisive breath. Hardly! That would get him a long way, he thought sarcastically. Instead of being impressed with the new David Anthony and welcoming him back into her life with open arms, he knew that Mariah Benedict would be totally disenchanted. He suspected she'd call him a liar and a cheat and tell him what he could do with his million dollars and his apartment complexes!

Mariah already believed that financing her business had been his way of buying her affection and attention. Damn it, maybe she was right! He wasn't worth the ground she walked on, he decided morosely, downing his wine in one swallow. He'd tarnished his integrity even in his own eyes. What an egotist he was! How in the hell could he ever have become obsessed with the crazy idea that every woman he met was after him for his money? With a stab of pain he remembered that in an intimate moment Mariah had once confided she'd been attracted by his back!

Rising, he took a bill from his wallet and laid a generous tip on the table before taking the check to the cash register. While he waited for his credit card to be returned by the cashier, he glanced into the dimly lit lounge that already held a few stool sitters at the bar although it was only early afternoon.

If he had done nothing else, he thought with a small measure of satisfaction, he'd at least helped Mariah get out of a line of work that she had wanted to be finished with and into a job she enjoyed.

Now his problem was to get her back into his life.

But a long month later, Mariah was still unyielding and unresponsive to David's ploys. One day she

163

asked Jeff to meet her on his morning coffee break, because she badly needed to talk with someone about her feelings, and Jeff was the only one she knew who would understand.

"I'm not sure it's healthy for me to meet you in public like this," Jeff quipped as he sat in the chair across from her at the coffee shop down the street from the bank.

"I went ahead and got you some coffee and a blueberry muffin," Mariah said. "Even with all the other kinds to choose from, blueberry is still my favorite."

"Mine, too." Jeff smiled, pulling the paper baking cup loose before taking a bite.

"What did you mean about meeting me not being healthy?" Mariah asked.

"I can't be sure Anthony won't burst in here any minute and get so jealous that he'll use me as a punching bag."

"He wouldn't do that!" Mariah exclaimed.

"Don't be so sure," Jeff answered cryptically. "How are things going between you two?"

"They aren't," Mariah said flatly, though she couldn't keep the sadness from creeping into her voice. "Unless he apologizes for his ridiculous accusations about you and me, David and I have no future. At times I'll admit I've been tempted to make the first move toward reconciliation, but I'm just not going to do it. None of what went wrong between us was my fault!"

"You're right there," Jeff agreed. "It can all be chalked up to Dave's hard-headed stubbornness."

"Well," Mariah took a sip of her coffee, "there's nothing I can do about that. And until he can come up with a logical explanation for doubting my faith-fulness I won't give in to my emotions."

Watching Jeff eat, Mariah realized she had no ap-petite and idly pushed her muffin away.

"You see," she explained earnestly, "I've forgiven him for deceiving me about the bank loan, I really have. It was wonderful of him to arrange to loan me money from his own personal account. I know how hard he's worked to get out from under the debts he was left with after the divorce. I suspect the whole affair may even have damaged his credit rating."

Watching Jeff choke on his last bite of muffin, Mariah asked solicitously, "Are you going to be all right?"

"Fine," Jeff managed to get out after clearing his throat a few times. "Just fine."

"You know, it's hard to believe," she mused aloud, "that after we'd known each other for only a day David was willing to put enough faith in me and my idea for a business to loan me over ten thousand dollars. And yet on the other hand, after we've been as intimate as two people can be for months, he's absolutely unwilling to trust my integrity in our per-sonal relationship. That's what really what ticks me off."

"Is that actually how long you'd known one an-other when he sent you to the bank?" Jeff asked incredulously.

"Yes. That was it."

"He never told me that. But then that guy never tells a lot of people the things he should," Jeff mut-tered.

"What was that?" Mariah asked. "I didn't catch what you said."

"It was nothing important," Jeff quickly assured her, placing his napkin on the table.

"It's all because of that damned ex-wife of his. That Carla," Mariah declared vehemently. She hesitated just a moment before asking, "What was she like, Jeff? You knew her. Was she beautiful?"

"She couldn't hold a candle to you," Jeff assured her sincerely.

"Are you sure?" Mariah asked. "Or are you just saying that to make me feel better?"

"I'm positive," Jeff reiterated. "But you asked what she was like. Let's see. Vain, self-centered, not beautiful, but so convinced she was, that until people came to know her well, she could make them believe it was true. You know the type I mean?"

"I think so," Mariah agreed, nervously worrying her lower lip. "I've known women who were so sure of themselves that just believing they were pretty was enough to almost make it so."

"You've got it," Jeff encouraged her. "That was Carla. She'll still think she's the cutest thing on two feet when she's having her third face lift."

"Has she already had one?" Mariah asked, her eyes widening.

Jeff chuckled. "I haven't seen her for a while, so I couldn't tell you. Maybe since her present husband is a doctor she can get cut rates!"

"Jeff," Mariah broke into his laughter with a stern note, "I didn't come here to make fun of Carla. She's only important to me because of the damage I think she's done to David. I wonder if he'll ever be able to trust another woman after she took him to the cleaners financially and made a fool of him with other men. And until he overcomes that humiliation to his damned male pride, there isn't anything more I can do to help him out of his misery.

"And he is miserable, Jeff. I can tell he's as miserable as I am. Each time I have to see him because of business, I can read the longing he feels for me written all over his face. It's all I can do to keep from throwing myself into his arms, I'm so anxious to kiss the hurt away."

"Don't do it," Jeff warned, placing some money in her palm to reimburse her for the snack she'd picked up for him at the counter. "David has to fight his own devils—come to his own terms. You've done everything you can. Everything you should do. If you give in to him your relationship will never last. Believe me. You have to be as strong and unrelenting as he is. Stronger even."

He rose, then bent to kindly brush her forehead with his lips. "Keep your chin up, kid. That big moose loves you. He'll come around if you play it cool."

Mariah sat at the table long after Jeff had left, thinking over the advice he'd given her. Instinctively she'd known this was the only path open to her. She couldn't make apologies for things she hadn't done any more than she could capitulate to David's wishes concerning her career. It hadn't been easy, but each time she'd encountered him, she'd managed to keep her face impassive even though her hands and knees shook terribly.

Mariah had kept David and the Superior Construction Company as clients, not only because they were two of her chief sources of revenue, but because she knew that on David's recommendation his boss had let the firm's secretary go on part-time pay, since Mariah had assumed many of her duties. And, she rationalized as she left the coffee shop, keeping David himself as a client had been a smart move. That way she could pay off his loan sooner with money that was directly coming from him! Somehow that knowledge seemed a sweet revenge.

The next day, driving toward Superior's construction site with a sheaf of electrical permits that needed David's personal signature as the crew foreman, Mariah cursed her luck that she would arrive too late to leave them in the office with the secretary. Julie left at noon and a glance at her car clock told her it was twelve fifteen. She would have made it in time, but Mrs. Bergstrom had baked an apple strudel that she'd insisted Mariah taste when she'd delivered her prescription. She knew Mrs. Bergstrom was lonely and enjoyed a few minutes' chat. It would have been rude to take a raincheck on the strudel, especially when she knew it had been baked just for her.

Driving through the apartment complex on the newly paved roads, Mariah finally spotted the crew of men working on a nearly completed structure. It was miraculous the way the spacious and distinctive buildings had mushroomed. The rawly bulldozed landscape that she'd first seen was now leveled and seeded with new green grass. Wide, curving sidewalks swept in front of the buildings, while fenced-in play yards in the back covered what had once been piles of rubble.

After pulling into one of the freshly painted and numbered parking stalls, Mariah went in search of David. When she spotted him directing the unloading of a truck full of appliances, she squared her shoulders and planted a professional yet distant smile on her face.

"Here are your electrical permits. They need to be signed and returned today." Mariah opened her briefcase and took out the papers. Holding the leather attaché case horizontal for a writing surface, she coolly looked away from the sight of his handsome face as her heart lurched painfully.

"Do you have a pen?" he asked, his deep voice stirring memories that threatened to weaken her will.

Raising her knee to support the case, she snapped it open and took out a pen. When she offered it to him their fingers touched. A shock as electrifying as though she'd touched a live wire ran along her nerve paths. Her knee lowered reflexively and the case spilled to the concrete, emptying its fluttering contents at her feet.

Quickly David bent and swept the papers together, then handed them to her, a knowing smile lighting his features.

It was several confused moments before Mariah could sort out the electrical permits from the rest of the papers which she stuffed unceremoniously back into the case.

Then defiantly thrusting the permits into David's hand, she let him find a writing surface to sign them on, resolutely holding her case by its handle at her side.

Mutely she waited, the pounding of her heart nearly audible in the silence.

When he'd signed the papers, he handed them back. Avoiding the unanswered question that his eyes always seemed to hold these days, Mariah

169

quickly took the forms from him and started back toward her car.

"Mariah," he called softly, although the effect of his voice on her senses was as though the word had pierced her back.

Stiffening, she turned. "Yes?" she asked.

"I have something I need you to do right away. Are you busy?"

"Of course I'm busy," she shot out testily. "I run on a tight schedule. Call my service and they'll make an appointment for you."

"But I need some money transferred to my personal account and I need some cash. I'm down to my last cent. It's Friday and I'll be working late tonight. Julie's already gone or I'd have her do it."

Sighing with resignation, Mariah said, "All right. Where are your withdrawal and deposit slips?"

"In my truck. Down there." He pointed down the hill toward the temporary building Julie used as an office. "Will you give me a lift?"

Knowing it would be ridiculous to refuse, Mariah nodded. But when he folded his rangy length onto the front seat of her compact car she was sorry. It would have been far better to have let him run in the street alongside her car than risk having her senses bombarded by his nearness.

In the confines of the vehicle her peripheral vision picked up the golden hairs springing from his tanned arms. Immediately she was reminded of the sensuous tickle of those soft bristles tantalizingly brushing her back as he held her in his arms. And the sight of his long sturdy thighs casually spread as he sat beside her took her breath away as she remembered the full force of their latent power. Even the subtle smell of

170

his aftershave played havoc with her susceptible senses.

The few blocks they traveled seemed to stretch forever as she nervously steered her car toward its goal. Braking in front of David's truck, she kept her motor running while she waited impatiently for him to get out, but he seemed in no hurry.

"Mariah." He spoke her name again with the same devastating effect his voice always managed to have on her. "Would you like to go away with me this weekend? We could talk and—"

"I'm busy," she interrupted, her hands tightly gripping the wheel. Did he think that all he needed to do was beckon and she'd come running? She wouldn't even listen to him until he began by saying he was sorry.

"This job is nearly finished and later this fall and winter I'll have plenty of time on my hands."

"Good, then you won't be needing my services any longer. I've been making double payments on my loan and I'll soon have you paid back."

It had been difficult sinking nearly every cent she'd earned into her indebtedness. She'd been back on her old spaghetti and noodle soup diet, saving out only what she needed for gas and rent ever since she'd learned that David was the one who held her contract. But it was worth the sacrifice to earn back her self-respect.

"I'll always need you," David said in a hoarse voice, raising his large hand to cover hers.

Flicking his hand away, she asked with all the non-chalance she could muster, "What for?"

Then, as all the possible answers he might be bold and brazen enough to give ran through her mind, she hastily added, "At your numerous requests, I've hired a service team to scour your apartment; cleaners to launder your rugs and upholstery; refinishers to restore your floors. I've taken every item of clothing you own to the dry cleaners and I've hired fumigators to look for roaches and termites. So you're all set.

"Please, will you just get your slips so I can go to the bank before I begin my afternoon schedule?" She kept her gaze focused straight out over the steering wheel, but to her dismay her voice had taken on a pleading tone.

Without another word, David got out of the car and opened the glove compartment of his truck.

Tears welled up in Mariah's eyes. In spite of the cloudy sky she opened her purse and took out her large-lensed sunglasses. By putting them on she hoped to hide from the exasperating man the visible sign of the mess he could make of her self-control.

Silently, Mariah took the banking slips David offered through the car window before she shifted into reverse and drove away from the complex without a backward glance.

By the time she reached the main branch of the bank after dropping off the signed permits, Mariah had her tears completely under control. Removing her sunglasses and drying the traces of dampness from her eyes, she thought of her afternoon. In spite of what she'd told David she had fewer jobs than usual this afternoon. She suspected there would be less call for gassing up cars now that summer was over. Even so, she'd have to hurry if she was going to get all the vehicles to the station and have the keys back to their owners before five.

As she turned into the bank's drive she noticed that all the parking slots were filled and that a group of well-dressed men had gathered in the parking lot. Even a portable TV van was on the spot. Had there been a hold-up? she wondered curiously as she circled the bank to join the line of cars waiting at the drive-up window. If so, it was business as usual she was grateful to note as an arm reached out from a car two vehicles in front of her to collect an envelope from the service drawer. Perhaps the local TV station was making some kind of documentary, she reasoned, as she watched a man with a hand-held camera sweeping the line of cars. She noticed a second man wearing a headset busily talking into the microphone of his portable transistor call radio.

Mariah inched her car forward as transactions were made for the customer in front of her. Then it was her turn to slide David's slips into the deposit drawer that had opened to accommodate her.

Suddenly, just as she touched the cool metal of the open drawer a deafening dinging of a high-pitched mechanical bell pierced the air. Automatically her hands flew to cover her ears. The man with the TV camera ran around the front of her car and forced his way between her car door and the drive-up window, his camera with its bright spot of light focused on her. The other man with the headset stuck a microphone into the open car window trying to shout over the ear-piercing din of the alarm.

Dear Lord! What had she done now? Mariah thought with panic, shutting her eyes tightly, not wanting to see the policemen she was sure were rushing to arrest her for some unfathomable crime.

173

Suddenly the alarm ceased, leaving an echo ringing in her head.

The loud voice of the man at her side demanded, "How does it feel to be the millionth customer of the Horace Higby National Bank?"

"I . . . I don't know," answered a stunned Mariah as the cameraman scrambled onto the hood of her car, aiming his lens at her through the windshield.

"Drive around to the front of the bank," the cameraman commanded from his perch on the hood. "There's a reception committee out there with your grand prize!"

"What's your . . . ?" the radioman called, running alongside her moving vehicle.

"I . . . I don't know," Mariah answered again, not having caught his question.

"Park here." He motioned her to a spot being vacated by the group of men she had noticed as she'd driven in.

Mariah obediently obeyed. Turning off her motor she shrank back from the men converging on her from all sides, several of whom were pointing cameras at her.

Then her car door was opened by unseen hands and she was graciously helped out by a stately white-haired man. As he calmly looked down at her Mariah felt her frightened confusion abate and her composure return.

"Allow me to introduce myself. I'm Joshua Hamilton, President of the Horace Higby National Bank and Trust Company," he stated with dignified solemnity.

"I'm Mariah Benedict, President of Procrastinators

174

Unlimited," Mariah declared, holding out her slim hand.

"Ms. Benedict," Mr. Hamilton said into a hand-held microphone while the group of men assembled respectfully around them, "the directors of the Horace Higby National Bank and Trust Company are proud to honor you as the one millionth customer to use our fully automated drive-in facility established five years ago in the city center for the convenience and security of our busy, time-conscious patrons. The unique feature of this particular service at our main branch is that each transaction conducted at the window is simultaneously transmitted to the main computer system where each account is immediately credited or debited according to the dictates of the transaction. This assures that customers using this facility will receive the benefits of our compound interest plan, computed daily."

Mariah tried to keep her mind on what the man was saying, but as the well-dressed men's eyes strayed during the speech from the bank president to her, she became acutely conscious of being dressed in the jeans and sweatshirt she customarily wore on Fridays when she gassed up clients' cars. Jamming her hands in her pockets, she decided that she couldn't help it if she wasn't dressed to suit these men's purposes, whatever they were. She gave up trying to make sense of her role in this whole scene, gathering only that it was some kind of publicity stunt.

"And so, Ms. Benedict, if you will kindly step over here, in the name of the Horace Higby Bank and Trust Company, the directors and I would like to present you with the keys to this vehicle."

The group parted and Mr. Hamilton led a dumb-founded Mariah to a low-slung cream-colored convertible. The top of the prestigious sports coupe was rolled back to reveal rich saddle-leather upholstery and bucket seats.

"This car? For me? You've got to be kidding!" Mariah exclaimed, taking her hands out of her pockets to reverently run her fingertips over the shiny finish.

"I assure you we're quite serious," Mr. Hamilton said.

"Thank you," Mariah stammered as he handed her a matching leather key case, lowering her eyes to cover her confusion.

She didn't know how to react. Should she behave like a contestant on a quiz show and jump up and down, squealing? Perhaps even kiss the dignified man's cheek? Just what was expected of her? Finally after a moment's pause she decided on a more restrained approach.

"Never in my wildest dreams have I imagined I'd ever own a car like this. Is it really mine? Just for being a customer?" she questioned hesitantly once again, her voice low and breathless with wonder.

"All yours, my dear," the bank president assured her, opening the door and handing her into the driver's seat, "as soon as you sign the registration and title. There are no strings attached. The directors have also provided a full tank of gas and ten days of insurance coverage to allow you to drive it from this spot immediately."

"I can't believe it!" Mariah dazedly shook her head, looking up at the smiling man.

Then a clipboard with several documents attached

176

was thrust before her and a slim gold pen placed in her hand.

"Sign here, and here, and here." A well-manicured finger indicated spaces that were marked in red ink with X's, "and record your address here."

Mariah did as directed and the clipboard and pen seemed to magically disappear.

"Would you like to take it for a little spin?" Mr. Hamilton asked, a twinkle in his eye as he exaggeratedly imitated a car salesman for the benefit of the rolling cameras.

"I don't even know where the key goes," Mariah answered, ducking her head down to search the dial-studded instrument panel of the two-seater.

"My wife has one just like it. Perhaps I can help you," Mr. Hamilton said as he walked around the powerful car and opened the passenger door. Once he was settled beside her, the bank president leaned over and put the key in the ignition.

When Mariah turned the key, the luxurious automobile purred to life. "Going my way?" she quipped, revving up the quiet motor.

"Most certainly, my dear."

With the TV van following them closely, Mariah drove the responsive car around the crowded city block, very aware of the curious stares of other motorists and pedestrians.

"I just can't believe this," Mariah remarked as much to herself as to her passenger. "It seems like a dream."

"I can imagine," Mr. Hamilton said, a broad smile lighting his features. "Speaking only for myself, I can't tell you how pleased I am that such an attractive young woman won this car. You look as if you belong behind the wheel, my dear."

Realizing the compliment was genuine, Mariah returned his smile. "Thank you. I'll try to take very good care of it."

"It should last a long time. Cars like this never go out of style and they hold their value. They're expensive, but a sound investment."

Mariah grinned. She felt more comfortable now that Mr. Hamilton was talking like a banker!

Once back in the parking lot of the bank, Mr. Hamilton and his directors turned Mariah over to the media, who questioned her intensely about herself and her business. Taking advantage of the chance for free publicity, Mariah answered expansively.

It was only when she glanced at her watch and she suddenly remembered her afternoon commitments that she begged off. A considerate TV crew member offered to drive her Supra to her apartment in exchange for a lift to the station.

After dropping him off Mariah couldn't resist the temptation to take a ride on the freeway that ran through the middle of the city to get the feel of the car and enjoy the marvelous sensation of her long hair streaming in the wind. For a few minutes she was determined to forget about David Anthony, the cars patiently waiting to be gassed, and the lonely weekend that loomed desolutely before her.

Turning on the radio, Mariah hummed along with the music, thinking that she had no use for two cars. She would no longer have to lease the Supra and those payments would go a long way toward paying off the remainder of her debt to David. Maybe there would be more to her future than peanut butter sandwiches and the hamburger casserole she'd planned for dinner!

But she hadn't gone many miles before a thought struck her that turned the happiness of the afternoon to ashes. It wasn't her car! Technically and ethically it was David's! She'd only been his proxy at the driveup window. He was the real customer and the real owner of the gorgeous convertible!

CHAPTER TWELVE

At the site of the almost completed apartment complex Mariah leaned on the horn of the convertible. She'd be damned if she'd search through the empty buildings to find David. A few more prolonged blasts brought the heads of several men to peer out windows and doors, but none of them was David's. Finally, one man who recognized her called down that David was over at the office.

Making a U turn in the deserted street, Mariah raced through the curving avenues to the makeshift building. Jamming the heel of her hand on the horn, she pressed it until David, holding a telephone receiver to his ear, came to the threshold of the open door. Mariah didn't stop honking until he hung up the phone and bounded out to the road.

"What's up?" he asked, his eyes taking in the car and its driver. "You look good in that. Gassing it up for a rich customer?"

Jumping from the car, Mariah threw the expensive leather key case at his chest and angrily stalked away.

"What the devil?" David asked, catching the keys with a fumbling grasp while he ran after her. When he reached her, he caught hold of her arm, turning her to face him.

"It's yours!" Mariah shouted.

"What's mine?"

"The car . . . the beautiful perfect car!"

"I never saw it before in my life," David objected, a frown furrowing his brow. "Where did you get it?"

"I got it at the bank. If you watch the five o'clock news on Channel 7 you'll get the whole story. Now let me go!" Mariah tried to wrench her arm free from David's tight grip.

"I'm not going to let you go until I hear the whole story—from you. Did you buy it?" He grasped her other arm and pulled her closer.

"Of course not! I won it—for being the zillionth customer or something like that. For a while I really thought it was mine until I remembered that I had gone to the bank for you! So it's yours, not mine." Humiliating tears of frustration and disappointment spilled over and ran down her cheeks. David was touching her, talking to her, looking with sympathy down into her face and yet he was out of her reach. She couldn't bear to realize that he didn't belong to her any more than the car did.

"Here," David said, sliding the hand holding the key case down her arm until he held it and her hand together in his. "Take them. The car is yours. If you were the zillionth person at the bank then there's no question about whose car it is."

"But I really wasn't the customer, you were!" she argued unreasonably.

"I'd have a hard time proving that." He chuckled. "I haven't left this place all day."

"The deposit slips would prove it," she argued obstinately.

181

"Okay. Okay, so the car is mine. But I'll only take it on one condition."

"What condition?" Mariah asked. Her hands held tightly at her sides, she leaned forward slightly, wiping the tears on her cheeks on the broad expanse of his T-shirt before raising her face to his.

"On the condition that the beautiful blonde who drove it over here comes with it. Otherwise, I don't want it."

Taking the keys pressed against her palm, Mariah angrily threw them down on the street. "Are you trying to buy me again?" she demanded.

"Damn it, woman, I love you," David bit out fiercely before he pulled her to him and enveloped her in the circle of his strong arms.

His fingers threaded through her hair as his demanding lips devoured hers, forcing open her mouth to the electrifying thrust of his tongue. The heat of his body permeated hers, causing a wave of fiery desire to wash over her as she lost herself in the ecstasy of his sensuous embrace. Her knees grew so weak she had to hang on to his broad shoulders to keep from sliding to the pavement. Still his relentless onslaught continued kindling her excited senses to flame. When she felt she couldn't hold on a second longer, his lips pulled away, leaving her gasping for breath. He continued to support her weight, holding her closely to the massive expanse of his heaving chest until their ragged breathing and beating hearts slowed a bit.

Gently stroking her tumbled mane of golden hair, David remarked, "I never thought I could buy you. There isn't that much money in the world. You mean more to me than anything money could buy."

Gently cupping her chin, he raised her face so that he could look into her eyes. "I only arranged for the loan because you were so disappointed that day. I wanted to do whatever I could to make you feel better."

"But I didn't want to take your hard-earned money. It makes me feel as though I've used you to get what I wanted. What if I hadn't made a go of my business? Where would you have been then? If I'd known it was your money, I'd never have taken it. You didn't give me that choice." Mariah was inclined to argue further, but looking up into his dear face she knew she only wanted to feel the thrill of his lips against hers once more.

"Honey, I could afford that loan. It didn't take anything out of my working capital. I wanted you to have a chance to find your own worth. You seemed so damned dejected about being on unemployment and I certainly didn't want you to go back to waitressing if you didn't want to.

"It was when your business started taking you away from me that I got a little hot under the collar." He lightly brushed her moist lips with his causing a shiver to run down her spine.

"But David, what about those terrible things you said about Jeff and me? He's never been anything but a perfect gentleman. In fact, he likes to talk about you!"

"I guess I'm just crazy in love with you. I've never felt this way about anyone in my life. After Carla I believed I'd never trust anyone again. I was a fool to let her continue to poison my life. I'm sorry for what I said, honey. I've been kicking myself about it for thirty-one awful days.

183

"I know I could never live with a jealous woman, but I'd never thought about what it would be like if the shoe were on the other foot. I promise I'll never turn green again. If you'll let me, I'll spend the rest of my life showing you how much I trust you and love you. Can you forgive a man who loves you beyond reason? Whose life means nothing without you?"

For a long moment Mariah looked deeply into David's eyes. He'd hurt her badly with his accusation. It had been the one terrible wound to her heart that had kept her from him these past weeks. Every time she'd thought of making up with him, the memory of his harsh allegation had stopped her. But hearing the words she'd longed to hear from him and understanding that he truly realized what he'd done to both of them by mistrusting her, Mariah forgave him with all her heart.

She sighed, then answered very seriously, "Yes, David, I do forgive you." As she spoke the words she felt the pain lift from her heart and joy fill her being. With a complete and unequivocal surrender to her love for him, Mariah raised her arms to encircle the strong column of his neck.

She inclined her head slightly forward, intent on what she had to say. "There is one more thing, David. About my business—"

"Honey, I'm proud of you and your business," he interrupted.

"It's not a harebrained scheme?"

David visibly grimaced. "It's not a harebrained scheme. You've succeeded beyond anything I thought you could have done with it. There isn't another woman in Seattle who could have done what you've done," he declared expansively. "There isn't

184

another woman who could do justice to that fabulous automobile you just won, either. And there isn't another woman who could fit so perfectly into my life and my dreams for the future."

"I have a dream for our future too. My business is expanding and I don't want to give it up. I'm tired of living on a shoestring. I'm tired of wearing second-hand clothes. I'm tired of spaghetti every other night," she wailed. "My whole adult life has been like that. I want us to have more."

"It's time you got that assistant you were talking about," David said. "You can hire people to do the leg work for you while you become an executive with reasonable hours. You need to leave a little time for your husband."

"And where will that leave me with you working six days a week every waking daylight hour? How about some time for your wife?"

David's face took on a strange look. "Mariah, I haven't been honest with you about that either. I own these buildings I've been working so hard to finish. And when we're married they'll be yours too. In fact we own several other complexes, including the one I'm living in now. Tonight I'll take you on a grand tour of all the real estate that will soon have your name added to the deeds."

"Are you trying to tell me you're rich?" Mariah shrieked. "That you don't have to stand out there in the sun pounding nails all day to make a living? That all those buildings are really yours? Is that what you're saying?" Mariah demanded, attempting to pull back from the pressure of his arms. "I can't believe it! Why didn't you tell me that right from the start? I feel like a fool!"

"You're no fool," David interjected quietly. "If anyone's a fool I am. You see, you fell in love with me thinking I was a working man and I was afraid that if you knew, things would change between us. I was going to tell you that night you stormed out of my apartment. I was going to tell you that you didn't need to work, that I had more than enough for us."

"This is going to take some getting used to," Mariah protested weakly. "I'm not sure I'm hearing right. Are you the big boss? The owner? The slave driver?"

"That's me," David confessed with a smile. His face took on an earnest expression. "Mariah, you've got to understand. I've worked all these years waiting for you to come into my life. I knew you were out there somewhere. What I didn't know was that I was going to find you standing right behind me in a line at the license bureau. I'm so glad I found you, honey."

Mariah tore her gaze from his, her eyes sweeping the curving rows of apartment houses surrounding them. "Honestly? These are all yours?" she asked again, incredulously.

"Ours," he corrected. "And to prove it, I've hung up my tool belt for the last time. I'll never put it on again."

His tender gaze caressed her eyes while his warm breath swept her cheek. With lips still parted in astonishment she waited for his slowly descending mouth to reach hers. His kiss was as gentle as velvet, and so sweet she felt her doubts and fears fade away as love for David saturated her senses.

In a daze she felt his lips leave hers. Keeping one arm around her, he stooped to pick up the keys on the pavement.

"Your keys," he said, handing them back to her. "Come on, let's go for that ride now. You drive. We'll ride off into the sunset together." Squeezing her shoulder, he chuckled happily.

Walking her back to the car, he held her tightly to him, matching his stride to hers.

Once behind the wheel of her dream car, reality penetrated Mariah's dream world like a bolt of lightning.

"I can't drive off into the sunset yet," she moaned. "I've got six cars to gas up before five o'clock."

"We'll get the parking lot attendants to do it this time."

"And I didn't get your money! It's still at the bank!"

"I've got a card for the cash machine."

"You think of everything, don't you?" Mariah purred, settling back against the luxurious leather seat.

"Right now I've got only one thing on my mind," David said, leaning his broad shoulders toward her and pulling her close. His hand slid beneath her sweatshirt and cupped her breast, his fingers teasing the erect nipple beneath her filmy bra, as his mouth drew from hers another long, lingering kiss before she determinedly started the engine.

Doggedly driving from one parking garage to another at Mariah's insistence, the tension between them mounted almost unbearably. She could have been driving the old beater she'd had when she'd first met David for all the awareness she had of the fantastic convertible carrying David and her through the streets of the city. Her thoughts and sensations were only for the incredibly compelling man beside her.

She longed to touch the hair that curled at his nape, yearned to run her hands over the rippling muscles of his back, craved to feel his long legs entwined with hers. She hardly dared look at him for fear her smoldering desire would erupt through her barely controlled composure.

By the time they reached her apartment building her composure had disintegrated to the point where she could scarcely climb the three flights of stairs. Supported by David's strong arm, urged on by his undisguised ardor, Mariah breathlessly made it to the top landing. Fumbling in her purse, she found her key and handed it to him.

After the door had closed behind them, he gathered her to him with an urgency that matched her own. Slipping his hands beneath her shirt, he unhooked her bra, and with one smooth motion slid her shirt over her head and flung it unceremoniously to the floor. Then he was on his knees, his face buried in her exposed breasts as his hands unbuttoned her jeans. Again with another single motion he freed her body from her bikini, jeans, and shoes. His large frame shook as his mouth descended over hers, his tongue savagely plundering its depths as his hands ran down the length of her supple back, melding her to his heated length.

Locked tightly to him, she plucked at the fabric covering his shoulders, mutely imploring him to remove his shirt, to remove his pants, to give her the pleasure of his muscular body.

He pulled away long enough to comply. With Mariah's help, in a few movements his muscular body was unclothed and ready to satisfy her ravenous need.

Swinging her up in his arms, he carried her to the white fluffy throw rug in front of the couch and carefully laid her down, poising above her only long enough for his hands to trace the fullness of her high breasts, her shapely waist, the sweet swell of her womanly thighs before he covered her body with his, his flesh touching, burning into every inch of her.

"I love you, Mariah," he said brusquely, his voice hoarse and taut with passion. His hands slid beneath her buttocks to cradle her undulating hips as his mouth sought hers languorously, erotically, kissing her fully.

Her fingernails dug deeply into his muscular shoulders as he entered her, filling her being with a vibrancy that pulsed with a driving heat. Mariah clung to his heaving body. Arched tightly against him, she matched his thrusts with a driving need of her own to possess this man as totally and completely as he possessed her.

Together they reached a shattering climax, each calling to the other in their ecstasy. They were bonded, forged forever in the ultimate intimacy they would share throughout their years together.

When at last the rising sun intruded on the hours of mutual loving that had filled them with satisfaction, Mariah stirred. Cuddled next to David's sleeping form, she softly kissed his shoulder, tasting the salty tang left on his skin from his passionate exertion.

"David? David?" She said his name dreamily, wondering if the almost unfathomable events and disclosures of the day before could possibly be real.

"Umm?" came the groggy reply.

"Do you know what's happened to me?"

"Uh-uh," was the muffled response.

"Unless I'm dreaming—and if I am I don't ever want to wake up—I've won a car, I've got my man, and I've got the right to be a full partner in my marriage. David, wake up, please! Am I dreaming?"

"Not unless I am too," he murmured, stirring to burrow his face in her neck, circling his moist tongue around the outline of her ear.

"What more could any woman want?" she asked as he turned his chiseled face toward hers.

"I'm sure, given time, you'll think of something," he teased.

"David, this is serious!" Mariah protested, trying to ignore his hand on her breast. "We need to talk."

"You talk, honey, I'll listen," David replied, taking her hardened nipple in his mouth.

"David . . . David," she called his name softly. "Actually, when I think about it there is just one more thing . . ." She hesitated, wondering if it was tempting fate to ask for more.

His chuckle was deep. "And what might that be?"

"Well, would you mind not hanging your toolbelt up quite yet?" she asked.

"I thought you didn't like me working the hours of a framer and carpenter. I thought I'd name someone to take my place on the next construction job," he answered, rolling over to take her into his arms.

"I'd like you to build just one more thing," Mariah said, her eyes shining with hope for their future. "A house for us and our children." She waited expectantly for David's reply.

He grinned. "When I said I would hang my toolbelt up for good I knew my fingers would occasionally itch for the handle of a hammer, or the feel of a level."

"Then you'll do it?" Mariah asked, unable to conceal her childlike glee.

"Of course I will, honey. Actually," he admitted, "I'm miles ahead of you. I've had an architect working on some alternate sets of plans. I wasn't sure whether you'd want to live in the city, or in the suburbs . . . whether you'd want some acreage or a view . . . or both. I've had my eye on some possible sites. I've just been waiting for the lady of the house to make those decisions. I'll leave everything except the actual materials that I use to construct the house to you." He gazed into her eyes. "That is, if you like beamed ceilings and lots of cedar and white stone."

"I love them." Mariah sighed, her happiness complete. A new thought struck her. "David, what about children?"

"That's up to you too, sweetheart, as long as you promise me a girl that looks just like her mother."

Mariah circled her arms around David's neck and pulled his lips just a breath from hers. Locking her gray gaze with the green of his, she said, "No problem, as long as you give me a boy that's the spitting image of his dad."

"I'll get on it right away," David promised with a boyish grin, pulling her warm length close to his.

"Which, the house or the baby?" Mariah giggled.

"One thing at a time, honey," was David's amused reply as his lips claimed hers.